From *Briny Candles*

"Will you act the ghost, Cousin? You ought to know how they are supposed to behave from those ghost stories you are continually reading."

"But they will recognize me," objected James. "I cannot make myself look like anyone else, you know that. The Basic Principle of Ultimate Truth imposed upon our Order absolutely forbids it. Whoever heard of a ghost who looked like someone else?"

"Very true," whispered Charles, "but there is no Basic Principle against putting a sheet over your head. Take one off your bed."

"And what will you do, Charles?"

"I will improve the occasion in divers ways. Leave it to me. Off with you, it is—it is the appointed hour!"

Back in the dark shadow under the stairs nobody noticed that James was no longer there. The silence became eerie, and when the fire slipped and fell together everyone jumped.

The hush was broken by Orleby-Appleton. "Is this part of your show, Pullinger? Or is the little beast real?"

There was a small monkey standing upright on the bar. He was dressed in a jacket and cap and could be seen quite plainly in the blue glimmer from the bar light. He had in one paw a glass of port from which he was slowly drinking, in the other paw he held the end of his own tail, a pose uncannily reminiscent of an Edwardian lady holding up the skirt of her long dress. Pullinger came across the room with quiet strides and the monkey bowed politely. Pullinger obviously did not believe in ghostly monkeys who drank port; he came steadily on and made a snatch at the animal. Even as his fingers closed upon it there was nothing there except the empty wineglass which was left in his hands.

The landlord leaned heavily upon the bar and addressed Secretary Pullinger in tones suitably low but nonetheless incisive.

"Monsieur. It is with delight that I entertain your group and provide food, drink, and accommodation. But it must be clearly understood that you entertain your ghosts elsewhere. What? If you were a football team you would not expect to kick your ball about in my house? I cannot permit that you play your ghost games here."

Books by Manning Coles

Ghost books
Brief Candles, 1954
Happy Returns (English title: *A Family Matter*), 1955
The Far Traveller (Non-series),1956
Come and Go, 1958

The Tommy Hambledon spy novels
Drink to Yesterday, 1940
A Toast to Tomorrow (English title: *Pray Silence*), 1940
They Tell No Tales ,1941
Without Lawful Authority, 1943
Green Hazard, 1945
The Fifth Man, 1946
Let the Tiger Die, 1947
With Intent to Decieve (English title: *A Brother for Hugh*), 1947
Among Those Absent, 1948
Diamonds to Amsterdam, 1949
Not Negotiable, 1949
Dangerous by Nature, 1950
Now or Never, 1951
Alias Uncle Hugo (Reprint: *Operation Manhunt*), 1952
Night Train to Paris, 1952
A Knife for the Juggler (Reprint: *The Vengeance Man*), 1953
All that Glitters (English title: *Not for Export*;
Reprint: *The Mystery of the Stolen Plans*), 1954
The Man in the Green Hat, 1955
Basle Express, 1956
Birdwatcher's Quarry (English title: *The Three Beans*), 1956
Death of an Ambassador, 1957
No Entry, 1958
Concrete Crime (English title: *Crime in Concrete*), 1960
Search for a Sultan, 1961
The House at Pluck's Gutter, 1963

Non-Series
This Fortress, 1942
Duty Free, 1959

Short Stories
Nothing to Declare, 1960

Young Adult
Great Caesar's Ghost (English title: *The Emperor's Bracelet*), 1943

Brief Candles

Manning Coles

with an introduction by
Tom & Enid Schantz

The Rue Morgue Press
Boulder, Colorado

Contents

Introduction   7
Frontispiece   10
Chapter I: 1870   11
Chapter II: 1953   18
Chapter III: Calm Yourself, Jules   25
Chapter IV: Trouble at the Bank   33
Chapter V: Bells of Shandon   40
Chapter VI: A Pair of Jokers   48
Chapter VII: Ulysses   57
Chapter VIII: The Lottery Ticket   66
Chapter IX: A Matter of Passports   74
Chapter X: Roux Dances   83
Chapter XI: The Guillotine   88
Chapter XII: Nice Women   98
Chapter XIII: Ointment for Bruises   107
Chapter XIV: Traffic Jam   114
Chapter XV: The Ghost-Hunters   121
Chapter XVI: Cold Hands   130
Chapter XVII: Rue Caumartin   137
Chapter XVIII: Key Ring   145

To **E.M.S.** *who detests spy-thrillers*

INTRODUCTION
A Happy Collaboration

MANNING COLES was the pseudonym for two Hampshire neighbors who collaborated on a long series of entertaining spy novels featuring Thomas Elphinstone Hambledon, a modern-language instructor turned British secret agent. Most of Hambledon's exploits were aimed against the Germans and took place from World War I through the Cold War, although his best adventures occurred during the Second World War, especially when Tommy found himself, for one reason or another, working undercover in Berlin.

Some of those exploits were based on the real-life experiences of the male half of the writing team, Cyril Henry Coles (1899-1965), who lied about his age and enlisted under an assumed name in a Hampshire regiment during World War I while still a teenager. He eventually became the youngest officer in British intelligence, often working behind German lines. After the war, Coles first apprenticed at John I. Thorncroft shipbuilders of Southhampton and then emigrated to Australia where he worked on the railway, as a garage manager, and as a columnist for a Melbourne newspaper before returning to England in 1928.

The following year his future collaborator, Adelaide Frances Oke Manning (1891-1959), rented a flat from Coles' father in East Meon, Hampshire, and the two became neighbors and friends. Educated at the High School for Girls in Turnbridge Wells, Kent, Manning, who was eight years Coles' senior, worked in a munitions factory and later at the War Office during World War I. In 1939 she published a solo novel, *Half-Valdez*, that failed to sell. Shortly after this disappointing introduction to the literary world, Coles and Manning hit upon an idea for a spy novel while having tea and began a collaboration that would last until Manning died in 1958. Coles continued the Hambledon series for an additional three books before he died in 1965.

The Hambledon books, especially the first two, *Drink to Yesterday*

7

and *A Toast to Tomorrow* (*Pray Silence* in England), were great successes. Published in 1940 in England and 1941 in the U.S., the two books almost immediately went into large reprint editions. This was a most unusual circumstance during the early years of World War II when anti-German sentiment was at its height, given that the books, while denouncing Naziism, presented a balanced, sympathetic and often laudatory portrait of the German people, who the authors said had been betrayed and deceived by all sides following World War I. Yet there is never any question as to Hambledon's loyalties. "If a country is worth living in," he said, "it is worth fighting for."

Those first two Hambledon adventures were chosen by Howard Haycraft for his list of cornerstone mysteries in his 1941 study of the genre, *Murder for Pleasure*. Critic and fellow mystery author Anthony Boucher said the two volumes should be treated as one book, "a single long and magnificent novel of intrigue, drama and humor." Most of the humor, however, is to be found in the second volume. *Drink to Yesterday* is a realistic and often grim look at war and the effect it has on the ordinary people who have to fight it. Readers would do well to immediately read the first few pages of *A Toast to Tomorrow* after finishing *Drink to Yesterday* to enjoy one of the greatest jokes ever played out on the pages of a mystery novel. If you haven't yet made the acquaintance of the Tommy Hambledon books, you should avoid reading the next paragraph—we wouldn't want to spoil the fun.

When *Drink to Yesterday* closes, it appears as if Tommy may have been killed in the line of duty while undercover behind enemy lines. When he's discovered, still alive and carrying forged but very convincing papers that identify him as Klaus Lehmann, the amnesiac Tommy is naturally assumed to be German and is repatriated to his "home" where, thanks to his fluent German and skills learned as an agent, he is able to rise to the position of Chief of Police in Berlin as Hitler comes to power. On the eve of World War II, Tommy's memory returns and he immediately offers his services to the very surprised—and pleased—British Secret Service. For the rest of the war, Tommy takes on German saboteurs and fifth columnists. He returns to Nazi Germany in *Green Hazard*, perhaps the second best book in the series, to rescue an anti-Nazi scientist who has invented a powerful new explosive. After the war, Tommy continues to serve England but the series never again reached the level of entertainment achieved in those first few books, although Boucher described them as being filled with "good-humored implausibility."

That same good humor—and a good deal more implausibility—is to be found in the collaborators' four ghost books, which began with the present volume, *Brief Candles*, in 1954, and included two other books featuring the ghostly Latimers, *Happy Returns* in 1955 (published in England as *A Family Matter*) and *Come and Go* in 1958. A fourth ghost book, *The Far Traveller*, which features a displaced, displeased and deceased German nobleman who finds a movie company employing people of the most common sort invading his castle, appeared in 1956. Although the books were quite popular and appeared in the U.S. under the Coles byline, they were published in England under yet another pseudonym, Francis Gaite. Boucher described this new venture "as felicitously foolish as a collaboration of (P.G.) Wodehouse and Thorne Smith."

But the Coles' ghost books owed a lot more to the comic antics and social satire of a Wodehouse novel than to the malicious spirits who haunted Topper in Smith's novels. Deliciously spiteful in the novels, George and Marian Kirby were far more benevolent in the many movie and television versions, although, like the Latimers, they couldn't resist playing a ghostly practical joke or two on some stuffed shirt or larcenous intruder.

Emboldened by strong drink, Englishman James Latimer and his younger American cousin Charles shuffled off this mortal coil when they made a valiant but ill-advised attempt to resist invading Germans while visiting a small French village in 1870 during the Franco-Prussian War. The two can return to the world of the living only when one of their descendants is in trouble and close at hand. Sometimes this occurs by chance, as in *Brief Candles*, and sometimes through complicated intercessions, as in *Come and Go*, when Richard Scorby is induced, with the help of a medium and other subterfuges, to the village of St. Denis-sur-Aisne where the earthly remains of his ancestors and their port-drinking monkey Ulysses are buried.

Brief Candles is more episodic than subsequent books and reads almost as if the authors had intended it to be a one-shot affair. And although the Latimers outwit several criminals and murderers who unwisely cross their ectoplasmic paths, the book contains fewer mystery elements than do subsequent titles, which were published as mysteries in England and as "novels" here in the United States. The ghost books ended with Manning's death, and one can only hope than the two collaborators are having as much fun in the next world as they gave readers in this one.

Tom & Enid Schantz
Boulder, Colorado
January, 2000

The family of
LATIMER

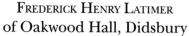

FREDERICK HENRY LATIMER
of Oakwood Hall, Didsbury

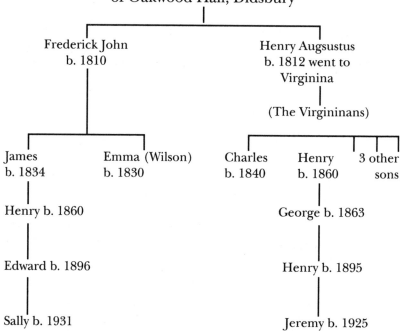

Frederick John
b. 1810

Henry Augsustus
b. 1812 went to
Virginina

(The Virgininans)

James
b. 1834

Emma (Wilson)
b. 1830

Charles
b. 1840

Henry
b. 1860

3 other
sons

Henry b. 1860

George b. 1863

Edward b. 1896

Henry b. 1895

Sally b. 1931

Jeremy b. 1925

CHAPTER I
1870

"IN MY DAY," said the old waiter, tottering round the room, "in my day, I repeat, the Armies of France were not defeated. They conquered, they swept all before them. I do not understand what ill fate has befallen the Armies of France." He threw a contemptuous look at three French soldiers sitting together at a table in the corner with their rifles and equipment upon a long bench beside them. They were eating hungrily, but their heads turned at every sound coming from the road which passed the inn; it was one of the main roads to Paris. "It must be the men," said the waiter. "In my day, we had men in the Armies of France."

"And a man to lead them," said one of the soldiers, angrily jerking round in his chair and then turning back to his meal again.

"And, as you say, a man to lead them."

There were two men sitting at a table in the window, eating their meal and looking down at the traffic below, which was all going one way, towards Paris. Guns and their limbers, wagons full of wounded lying on straw, infantry steadily plodding with no spring in their step, cavalry with their once gay uniforms masked with dust. Dust over everything and hanging in a heavy cloud in the air; it came in at the open first-floor window at which the men were sitting and fell upon the tables, the food, their hair, their clothes, and their skin, until everything they touched was soiled and gritty. The men were civilians and gentlemen by their dress; their valises lay on the floor beside them. The elder, a man in his late thirties, was the stouter of the two; the younger was very tall and thin with lank dark hair, hatchet-nosed and impulsive in movement. On the back of his chair there sat a small Capuchin monkey dressed in a little red jacket and a round cap. The monkey was eating a peach, and the juice ran down his chin and dripped upon his jacket.

"That animal of yours," said the older traveler, speaking in English, "is making himself a horrid sloven with that peach."

The younger glanced over his shoulder. "My fault. I forgot to give him a napkin." He changed to French, perfectly fluent but with an accent unfamiliar to the old waiter. "Be so good as to bring me another

11

napkin. My friend here is in difficulties with his peach."

The waiter awoke with a start from his plainly dismal thoughts and hurried forward with a napkin upon a salver. The monkey saw him coming, dropped the remains of his peach upon the floor, and snatched off his little cap with a polite bow. The waiter shuddered but stood his ground; the younger traveler took the napkin with a word of thanks and proceeded to tie it round the monkey's neck.

"Tell me," said the elder traveler in fair French with a strong English accent, "the battle, it has taken place? It is already over?"

"It is already over," said the waiter, shaking his head, and with that his hands began to shake also and his arms and his whole body, so that he laid hold upon the back of a chair to steady himself.

"And where did they fight?"

"Monsieur, at a place called Sedan."

"And France—"

"Has been defeated, monsieur. Never was there such a defeat. They say our armies are surrounded and these whom you see passing by are merely the stragglers."

"Take heart," said the English traveler. "News is never so bad as the first rumors make it."

One of the soldiers rose from table and came to the window to look out over their shoulders. "The gentlemen," he said in a tired, angry voice, "are interested in the battle?"

The younger man, having finished the monkey's toilette, gave him another peach and turned round. "Of course we are," he said in his odd drawling French, "seeing that we have come out from Paris in order to view it."

"To view it? To view a battle? Does the gentleman know what he is saying?"

"Of course I know," said the traveler calmly. "In my country, if a gentleman desires to observe the course of a battle he is freely at liberty to do so. Why not?"

The soldier called upon his Maker and went back to his table, but the waiter asked politely what country had the felicity to number Monsieur among its citizens.

"America," said the monkey's owner. "Waiter, bring another bottle. No, not another bottle of claret—brandy this time. Have you a passable brandy? You will drink with us, your morale appears to me to need restoring."

The waiter went to get it and the Englishman spoke in a low tone. "I should not give him too much, Charles. I think he has been restoring his morale considerably already."

"What he wants," said the American, "is to get drunk and sleep it off. The defeat will not seem so serious when he wakes up. That is what I did when I heard that Grant had taken Richmond. It does help, Cousin James, it does help."

"I dare say that you are in the right," said his English cousin with a sympathetic sigh, though indeed his own reaction to the news of the fall of Richmond had been of thankfulness that the wretched war was now over and there would once more be American cotton to supply his empty, silent mills.

The waiter came back with fresh glasses and a dusty bottle of brandy. There was a heavy rumble of passing guns and the glasses shook on the table.

"The patron's grandfather laid this down in the year when the Emperor—my Emperor—broke the Austrians at Wagram. We may as well drink it, gentlemen, or the brutal Prussians will." He spat a curse upon the Prussians and withdrew the cork.

"The patron," said the Englishman idly, "he is not here?"

"He has gone to Paris for safety. Madame insisted. One understands. They have five daughters." He began to pour out the brandy, but his hand shook so much that the spirit ran out upon the table.

"Give it to me," said the American. "'Waste not, want not,' is a good saying." He filled three glasses and gave the old waiter one. "Down with it. That'll warm your courage for you. Cousin James, your health. Sir, this is very fine brandy indeed."

"It is in truth," said the Englishman. "Cousin Charles, your very good health."

The old waiter bowed to them both and sipped his brandy. It appeared to do him good; a little color crept into his face and his hands steadied.

"Are you, then, alone in this place?" asked the man called James.

"Oh no," said the waiter. "There is my grandson in the kitchen. He cooks. There are also women who wash and clean and make beds, but today they have all run off to their homes. My grandson had the impertinence to tell me he also proposed to desert me, but I persuaded him to remain. With the spit. At present he is more afraid of me whom he knows than of the Germans whom he does not know—yet. He is green with terror, his hair stands on end and his knees shake, but he cooked the dinner. It was passable, yes?"

"Excellent," said the Englishman. "My compliments to him on that *ragôut*."

The waiter bowed.

"It needed a little more pepper," said the American.

"My fault, monsieur. His hand shook so much that I took the pot from him."

The monkey chattered angrily and his master looked round.

"He is thirsty," he said. "Waiter, a little wine and water for my friend."

"In a basin?" said the waiter, tottering away to the sideboard.

"Basin? No, why? In a glass, like a Christian. Do you think he has no manners?"

The waiter muttered something inaudible and brought back wine mixed with water in a thick glass.

"Thank the gentleman, Ulysses," said the American.

The monkey stood up on the back of the chair, took off his little cap with one paw, placed the other over his heart, and bowed deeply.

"Ulysse?" said the waiter. "That is, then, the little creature's name, Ulysse?"

"That is so. I named him after a certain general whom I had reason to dislike."

The Englishman laughed shortly and poured out three more glasses while the American handed the monkey his wine. "Careful, Ulysses. Do not spill it."

The monkey sat down again on his haunches, received the glass slowly in two careful paws, and began to sip it, rounding his great dark eyes at the waiter.

"He is indeed like a Christian! He enjoys his wine!"

"Surely he does, why not? Here's your glass, waiter, drink up and become young once more."

"I thank Monsieur. May I, then, propose a toast this time? *France! France!*" He drained the glass at one draught and the travelers raised their eyebrows.

"France," murmured the Englishman diffidently.

"The fair land of France!" cried the American in ringing tones. "May all her enemies perish!"

The monkey, imitative in this as in all else, raised his glass also and returned it to his mouth. One of the soldiers in the corner said: *"Dieu-de-dieu-de-dieu,"* under his breath and looked hastily away.

"Not so much traffic going by now," said James, the Englishman, and it was true. The rumbling and the tramping had ceased and the dust began to fall again upon the road from which it had risen.

"The Army has gone past," said the waiter somberly. "That miserable line of stragglers, of which you have just seen the last, is the remnant of the Armies of France. Oh, when I was young, we did not run from our enemies like this! We fought, we died in heaps, but we conquered!" He seized the brandy bottle and refilled his own glass, entirely forgetting the others. "Invincible, unconquerable, always victorious—"

This was a little too much even for the sympathetic Englishman. "There was," he said quietly, "a certain battle at a place called Water-loo— "

"I was there," cried the waiter, "I myself, seventeen years of age. I tell you, monsieur, that we should have won there also if it had not been for these damned Prussians."

The soldier nearest to them laughed harshly. "Messieurs, permit me to tell you that that is equally true of the battle of Sedan!" He picked up the bottle of *vin ordinaire* from his own table, set it to his mouth and drained the contents, dropped his head upon the table, and began to snore.

The American held the brandy bottle to the light and said that there was not much left, they might as well finish it. From the road outside there came the thud of galloping hooves and the musical jingle of ac-coutrements as a disorganized bunch of cavalry swept past and disap-peared from sight.

"Cuirassiers," said the waiter, peering over the travelers' shoulders.

"Sir, that will be the rear guard," said the American, refilling the glasses. "Very shortly now, sir, we may expect the vanguard of the victo-rious enemy." His hand was perfectly steady, but his speech was begin-ning to thicken. "One last toast, Cousin James, and you, what's your name, waiter. One last toast. Death to the enemies of France!"

They drank it, solemnly, almost tearfully, and suddenly without warn-ing the waiter began to sing in a high cracked voice.

"Allons, enfants de la Patrie!
Le jour de gloire est arrivé—"

"A little inappropriate for the occasion," murmured the English-man, but his cousin cut him short.

"What is that shouting I hear? Quiet, fellow! Listen—"

They leaned from the windows to see a half-grown lad come tearing down the street shouting that they come, they come, the Prussians, the Prussians——

The French soldiers in the corner scrambled to their feet, shaking their comrade awake. They did not wait to pick up their kit or even their rifles, but rushed out of the room, oversetting a table and some chairs as they went. They could be heard stumbling and plunging down the stairs, and the Englishman looked down into the street but did not see them come out.

"They have gone by the back way, Cousin," said the American with an angry laugh. "Cut off across the fields."

"Cowards, cowards," wailed the old waiter. "They have even abandoned their rifles."

"Wise men, in my opinion," said James with a slight hiccough. "Excuse me, Cousin. They may even live if they run fast enough." He got to his feet and staggered a little. "I believe I have drunk enough, Charles, what say you?"

"You have the right of it, James, but our waiter is still upon his feet, such as they are." Charles got up a little unsteadily and the monkey climbed down to stand beside him, reaching up for his hand like a child. "You fellow, what are you doing with those rifles?"

"Loading them, monsieur, loading them. What else would one do with a rifle when there are Prussians on the sacred soil of France?"

"Sir," said Charles, swaying slightly, "you are in the right and, sir, I honor you for it. Sir, I fought at Gettysburg and as a soldier I salute you."

"I hold a commission in Her Majesty's Yeomanry," said James, "but I am by no means positive that that entitles me to call myself a soldier."

"Surely, James, surely. At least you can load and handle a rifle." Charles thrust one into his cousin's hands. "Take that and load it. Here, put this cartridge bag about you. There is here equipment for the three of us; that should be sufficient."

James Latimer broke into one of his short barking laughs. "Sufficient for what? To drive the Prussians from France?" He examined the rifle carefully, took a cartridge from his bag, and loaded. "The weapon is unfamiliar in detail, but to one accustomed to machines it presents no insoluble problems."

"We may not be victorious, gentlemen," said the old waiter, "but some defeats are more glorious than victory. On, then, to glory! *Vive l'Empereur!*"

"Come then, gentlemen," said the American. "Forward to defeat if not to victory!"

"Forward, the Army of Latimer," said James. "It is very peculiar and quite unexpected, but, Cousin Charles, I am enjoying this. I suppose it is all a dream?" he added doubtfully.

"If it be," said Charles Latimer, "why, then, James, we shall soon awake."

They went down the stairs into the deserted silent streets. The houses were all closed and shuttered, no voices came to them, and they saw nothing but a frightened face or two peering from behind curtains. They tramped on, their footsteps muffled in the thick dust and their shadows lengthening before them on the long straight road away from Paris, three tall men, though one was bowed with age, and beside one of them the tiny figure of the monkey holding his hand like a child, running and skipping to keep up.

Presently there emerged suddenly from a side road a troop of Prussian cavalry riding two by two with their officer at their head. They turned towards the three men and came on at a steady trot, nearer and nearer, fifty yards away, forty yards, thirty——

"Cousin Charles," said James Latimer, "I think that these are the enemy, what say you?"

"Waiter," said Charles Latimer, "who are these who come?"

The waiter, whose head had been hanging, looked up, stiffened like a dog, and swung his rifle off his shoulder.

"The enemies of France!" he yelled, and fired straight at them. He missed the officer in front but brought down a trooper in the third rank. The officer bellowed an order and himself fired first; there was a series of loud explosions from the short Prussian carbines and the waiter pitched forward on his face and lay still. Charles Latimer stood upright for a moment and then his knees bent under him and he went down in a heap with the monkey whimpering and chattering on his body.

James Latimer was quite unharmed and had not even removed the rifle from his shoulder; one would say he had forgotten that he had it. He looked down at the two dead men and took off his hat. The officer rode up with one of his sergeants and dismounted.

"What is this nonsense?" he said in French. "What folly is this?"

"I think," said James slowly, "that the Army of Latimer has been defeated."

"What? You are a civilian. You must know that for a civilian to carry arms in wartime is punishable with death. French Army rifles, too! Sergeant, disarm this man. I will have no *francs-tireurs.*"

James gave up the rifle without protest; the officer stooped over the body of Charles, and the monkey flew at him and bit him in the wrist.

"You would, would you?" said the sergeant, and shot the monkey through the head.

"The bites of monkeys," said James calmly, "are said to be poisonous."

There was the sound of footsteps thudding in the dust as a stout black-clad figure came running along the road from the village with his long soutane flapping about his legs. The officer, winding a handkerchief round his bleeding wrist, waited until the priest came up to them.

"I came," gasped the priest, "to beg you to have mercy on this poor village——"

"You have come at the right moment," said the officer.. "These men were *francs-tireurs,* you see their rifles. They fired on us and killed one of

my troopers. Two of these men are already dead and the third is about
to die. Tell your villagers what happens to those who lift a finger against
the Prussian Army. Tell them that if just one more shot is fired I will
burn the whole place to the ground. Understand?"

"I will tell them. I have already told them and I will tell them again.
But these two gentlemen are not of our village, they are strangers——"

"And the third?"

"A poor old man of over seventy——"

"Old enough to know better. Since you are here, perhaps this gentleman requires your spiritual services before he dies. You may have two
minutes." The officer drew out his watch.

"My son," said the priest, addressing James Latimer," come aside
for a moment."

They walked a few paces away and spoke in low tones.

"Father," said James, "I am not of your Communion, I am an Englishman and a Protestant. Nevertheless, I have something to say. Listen."

He had spoken only a few words when the officer looked up from
his watch and gave an order to the sergeant. There was a small barn
beside the road; the sergeant led James towards it and set his back to
the wall while six of the troopers dismounted, lined up in the road facing him.

CHAPTER II
1953

"I DON'T THINK this is a very interesting part of France," said Sally Latimer.

"It's historical," said Jeremy. "If that helps," he added doubtfully.

"Not in the least. What is the difference between a green field where
a battle has been fought and a green field where no battle has been
fought?"

"Is this a riddle?"

"No. Historical buildings, yes. You can look round an ancient hall
and tell yourself that these very walls heard the voice of Cromwell or
Nelson or Queen Victoria——"

"Or Mickey Mouse——"

"Shut up. But what's in a field? Green grass, some hedges, and a
tree or two."

"Green flies," said Jeremy Latimer, "some toadstools, and a cow or
two."

"Are we composing poetry? On our left hand, some forty miles away, thank goodness, is Verdun. On our right, only some ten miles away, is Sedan. But in between——"

"Yes," interrupted Jeremy, "you didn't like Verdun, did you?"

"Fort Vaux," said Sally, and shivered. "Please don't remind me of it. Miserable, despairing place full of dead men's bones."

"I dare say these fields are if we only knew it, but we don't, so it's all right."

Sally looked about her at the rolling fields. "All different shades of green, some with cows and some without. Where is this main road you're looking for?"

"I think it's just ahead, must be around here someplace."

The Rolls-Bentley tourer slowed down and stopped at the road junction while its two occupants peered at the signpost. "Right, Sedan and Mézières. Left, Vouziers, Rheims' and Paris. You needn't worry about the map now." The big car nosed carefully on to the main road and turned left.

"What's this place we're coming to?" asked Jeremy.

"Chemery, and the next after that is St. Denis-sur-Aisne."

"All these villages," said Jeremy, slowing the car for the village street, "look the same to me. All single-string places with flat-fronted houses exactly alike unless some guy has gone mad and given his front door a coat of paint, and that doesn't often happen. Most of them haven't even put a dab of cement into the bullet scars. I know the Second World War's only been over eight years and what is eight years in the life of a nation, but one would think they might have done a little something if only to celebrate their parents' weddings. I don't know how any of them know where they live. I mean, imagine driving home from the local market town in the local bus after dark, how do you know where you get out?"

"Oh, come," said Sally, "one must be just. You might say the same thing about Streatham or Lower Norwood."

"I do," said Jeremy simply. "Well, that was Chemery; let's step on it to the next place. Where shall we dine? At Rheims?"

The big car purred on down the long straight road which had the usual double line of poplars turning out the silvery underside of their leaves in the evening breeze. St. Denis-sur-Aisne came into view in the distance, roofs and a church spire among trees. On the left of the road there was a small barn standing alone; the farm to which it presumably belonged was two hundred yards farther on. Just before they reached the barn the car's engine stopped suddenly and they coasted to a standstill at the side of the road.

"Odd," said Jeremy, frowning. "What's bitten you, Rollo?"

"We can't be out of petrol," said Sally; "we filled up at Montmédy. Besides, look at the indicator."

"Oh, it's not that. More like an ignition failure. Just a minute."

Latimer was, like most young men of his age, a reasonably good motor mechanic. He applied all the usual tests to locate the trouble, but entirely without result. Half an hour passed.

"I don't know what the trouble is," he said. "Petrol is going where it should go and no place else, the plugs are all sparking, and everything else seems to be in order. Seems to be. Any suggestions?"

"None, unless it's bewitched."

"Do you suggest I send for a *garagiste* or for the priest? I suppose there is a garage in this town?"

"There's a cinema, anyway," said Sally, indicating a gaudy poster on the wall of the barn beside them. "Look, they're doing *Gone with the Wind.*"

Jeremy groaned. "Nineteen thirty-nine was it? Or 1938? If the *garagiste* is as out of date as the film—"

A stout elderly Frenchman came across the field, making for the barn, and Jeremy addressed him.

"Good day, monsieur. Would you be so good as to tell me whether there is a *garagiste* in the village? My car has developed some mysterious trouble which I cannot myself locate."

The farmer came to lean over the hedge and say that there was, indeed, a *garagiste* of the most superior attainments in the village, everyone employed him. "Myself, I would not dare to advise you. I am a motorist myself, but only of a two c.v. Citroen. Not such an auto as that. Monsieur, I have never seen such an auto. One would have said that it was impossible for such a one to breakdown."

"So would I," said Latimer ruefully, "but I should have been wrong, as you see."

"Monsieur, I have a telephone at my farm there. Would it serve you if I were to ring up André at the garage and tell him to come out to you?"

"Monsieur," said Jeremy, "there is nothing I should like better, if you would be so good. Er—I must repay you the price of the call."

"But, naturally," said the farmer, and took the money. "I am, in any case, going home at once."

"Monsieur," said Sally with a dazzling smile, "your politeness exceeds all that I have ever read of your chivalrous nation. My husband was in despair, quite overcome."

The farmer took off his hat. "Madame has but to smile like that and she will find all France at her command. *Au revoir,* madame, monsieur. I go to the telephone."

He paused only to put some sacks he had been carrying into the barn and lock the door, and then went away with long heavy strides towards his farm.

"Charming," said Sally, "charming."

"Look, angel. Could you, do you think, without too much strain, go a bit easy on that girlish charm of yours? I don't want to cramp your style any, but we're here for a nice quiet tour, not a war. I don't want to have to put up wire entanglements round Rollo."

"The French aren't really like that, are they? I thought that was all just travelers' tales. It's not? Oh dear. Well, we can always hop in the car and drive away, can't we? I wonder how long this man will be in coming." Sally shivered suddenly.

"Not cold, are you? Put your coat on. You didn't take a chill last night, did you? We'll go straight to the hotel in this place and get a little drink."

"No, no, it's all right, darling. I'm not a bit cold. It's just that I don't like this place much, somehow. It's all right, but I'd rather be somewhere else."

"Cheer up," said Jeremy, "this isn't Verdun. I guess you're tired, that's all; we have certainly covered some ground since Monday." He fussed round her until presently a large ancient Panhard arrived bringing the garage proprietor from St. Denis.

He exhausted himself in praise of the Rolls-Bentley. He had seen photographs of such cars, but never, until today, had his hands upon one, and so on. Eventually he opened the bonnet and carried out much the same series of tests as Latimer had done, with exactly the same lack of result.

"But there is nothing the matter," he said, "except that she will not go."

"Brother," said Jeremy in his native tongue, "you're telling me."

"Monsieur is English?"

"American."

"Good. Very good. Excellent. Now, about the auto. I can do no more here. I suggest that I tow Monsieur to my garage. I cannot do anything tonight—it is late, and besides, I have promised to take a little lady to the cinema." He jerked his head towards the poster. "It is good, they tell me. A long film, though, it is necessary to be in time, and I shall have the hair torn from me if I am late." He glanced at Sally. "Monsieur understands."

"Perfectly. But is there a passable hotel here to which I can take

Madame? We meant to sleep at Rheims."

"The Hôtel du Commerce, monsieur, is excellent. It is famous. The cuisine—people come from miles around to eat at the Hôtel du Commerce. It is clean, comfortable, and well furnished. Only last year there were two bathrooms put in and the sanitation completely modernized."

"Incredible," said Jeremy, and meant it. "Well, that settles it, we will go to the Hôtel du Commerce. But listen, I want to be away early in the morning, by nine o'clock if possible. We are for Paris."

"I myself," said the *garagiste*, "will be up at six and already working upon your auto."

They were towed the couple of miles to St. Denis and stopped at the Hôtel du Commerce to unload their luggage. There is inevitably a certain loss of dignity in being towed, and the more magnificent the towed car, the greater the loss of dignity. By the time they reached the hotel Sally was struggling with an attack of giggles.

"What's the matter, honey?"

"Nothing—only this makes me feel as though my knickers were coming down—"

"They aren't, are they?"

"No, no. Not really. It just feels like what I'd feel like if they did."

"It's Rollo who's losing his pants," said Jeremy grimly.

A little later, while people were assembling outside the cinema to await its opening, two men strolled down the street looking interestedly about them. They aroused a certain amount of interest in those who saw them, for their dress was markedly old-fashioned and both wore side whiskers of a curling luxuriance unknown to the present day. The older and stouter of the two had his hair and mustache neatly trimmed, but the younger, taller and thinner, wore his long enough to descend upon his collar and both ends of his remarkable mustache could be seen from behind.

"Look! Who are they?"

"Here come the most peculiar strangers! Where have they come from?"

"It is some fancy-dress."

"I have it. They are dressed in that manner to advertise this film."

"Without doubt that is it. These Americans, what will they not think of?"

"Maman! Maman! What is the matter with those men's faces? Maman. What is it that they wear all that fur for? Are they Russians? Maman!"

"No, no, *chéri*. They are only, as one might say, play-actors."

"Oh. Maman, where have they come from? Where have they come

from? Maman, where have——"

"Quiet, quiet, my child! They are to do with the cinema, that is all. Look now, the doors are opening."

The crowd pressed towards the doors and lost interest in the strangers, who strolled on together.

"We seem to be attracting a deal of attention," said the elder.

"So I observe," said the other. "Formerly I should have been gratified, but now I am not so sure." He twirled the ends of his long mustache. "My facial adornments have been admired in their time, but——"

"But I am not sure that the emotion aroused now is admiration, Cousin. A tendency to titter, perhaps?"

"Our clothes, too, are not such as are worn in these days. No, sir, we do not look like other men."

"I told you," said the elder anxiously, "that we made a mistake in coming out by daylight."

"And I tell you again, Cousin James, that your ideas are hopelessly old-fashioned. You, sir, have been reading ghost stories."

James nearly blushed. "Most men have their foibles," he said apologetically.

"I think we had better retire and discuss this matter in private."

"You are in the right, Charles. We cannot go abroad this, it will never do. We want to see the world, not to provide it with a rare show in our own persons."

They walked on slowly.

"Cousin James, what do you imagine that all those people were crowding to see?"

"Some acting, I presume?"

"We might go and see for ourselves, perhaps?"

"Not tonight," said James firmly. "We have more urgent fish to fry tonight. A tailor and a barber, by Jove."

They turned a corner into a side street and were lost to sight.

Gone with the Wind came to its appointed end and the audience went home to their beds. The streets were empty and the full moon shone down upon closed shops and darkened houses; only the Hôtel du Commerce showed lights in its windows, for the late train from Paris was not yet in and there might be travelers seeking accommodation. Only Jules Boulestier, the policeman, was still active, if that term can justly be applied to one half asleep on a bench under the dusty plane trees in the *place*. It was his tiresome lot to be on duty three nights a week until the eleven forty-five from Paris had come in, but that did not mean that a stout elderly man within easy fetch of his pension need exhaust himself unnecessarily. He turned upon the hard bench, rested his arm along the back, and sighed deeply. He had visited one or two café's earlier in the evening and his head ached. Perhaps it would be as well to let the effects of his visits wear off before he went home to his wife. A good woman, Marthe, but what a tongue! Like a two-edged razor. As though a little brandy ever—

A soft padding sound came to his ears and he opened his eyes unwillingly. If that was the postmaster's geese which had got themselves loose again Boulestier would simply not see them. A policeman is not a goose-herd. He saw something moving along the road and lifted his head sharply.

The moonlight dripped through the leaves of the plane trees and made a shifting, deceptive pattern upon the road and the houses before him. Two dim figures were passing him only ten paces away; they were indistinct, but he could see them well enough. Two men, one tall and thin, the other rather stouter, and they were completely naked, even barefoot. Their white bodies shone faintly in the moonlight.

"It is the brandy," murmured Boulestier. "Marthe was right. She told me I would see things and I do. Naked men do not—"

At that moment one of the dim figures appeared to tread upon something sharp. It stumbled, and there came to his ears a sound like an imprecation. Its companion took it by the arm and it went on, limping.

Boulestier rose from his seat. Illusions do not stub their toes. He crept after them, keeping in the shadow, and argued within himself.

"It does not matter," said his worse self. "There is nobody about, and so long as they make themselves scarce before the passengers come from the train there is no harm done. Sit down again, poor tired Jules, and let the gentlemen enjoy themselves in their own way."

"Shame on you, Jules Boulestier, servant of France," said his better self. "Have you, then, worn the uniform of the police for thirty-four years and seven months to neglect your duty now? This village is in your charge; will you permit it to be infested with nudity?"

"Careful," said his worse self. "Perhaps they are escaped lunatics. Lunatics do tend to undress themselves, for they have no modesty. Besides, as everyone knows, they have the strength of ten. Do you, then, wish your wife to become your widow?"

"Duty, Boulestier, duty," urged the nobler voice. "If you are indeed slain in the performance of your duty, what a funeral you will have!"

The dim white forms had reached the shops and were apparently window shopping; they drifted from shop to shop wherever the blinds were not drawn. They reached the great establishment of Aristide Vigneron et Cie., a shop where one could buy anything from clothing to mousetraps. Aristide Vigneron was the Selfridge of St. Denis; he had no less than five windows in a row and the entrance was an arcade leading back from the pavement. The white figures turned into this arcade and naturally passed out of Boulestier's sight. He straightened his trembling knees and followed them.

When he reached the arcade and peered cautiously within, there was no one there. He steadied himself with a hand against the glass and went in. The double doors were shut, as they should be at this time of night; he tried them and they were securely locked. He turned his torch upon them and noticed that a spider had laid its web across from one bronze handle to the other.

Boulestier went back to his seat under the trees and held his head in his hands.

"What I want," he said aloud, "is a drink. A large cognac."

"At least," said his better self consolingly, "at least, Jules, you did not funk it."

CHAPTER III
Calm Yourself, Jules

THE PARIS TRAIN came in, deposited half a dozen passengers, and went on its way. The passengers came through the village towards their various beds; they were all known to Boulestier and he saluted them, especially the village priest.

"A fine evening, Monsieur le Curé."

"Aha, Boulestier! Still at the post of duty?"

"Naturally, monsieur."

"Good man, good man. Good night."

"Good night, monsieur."

Boulestier stretched his arms and yawned happily; now he could go home to bed. He had managed to persuade himself that the episode of the naked men had been merely a vivid dream, though it was odd that the memory of it did not begin at once to fade after the manner of dreams. He walked down the road towards the establishment of Aristide Vigneron; dream or no dream, he could not pass it close, upon the pavement. He made a detour into the road, under the trees, and just before he reached it two men came out from the arcaded entrance. Boulestier stopped dead; the two men walked away from him.

"It is all right, Jules," he muttered to himself. "These are not the same two. For one thing, they are fully dressed. Calm yourself, Jules."

They were not only fully dressed but they carried raincoats over their arms and each had a suitcase. They went on and Jules hurried after them. The taller of the two evidently heard him coming, for he glanced round and touched his companion upon the arm. They mended their pace and turned at the next corner. Boulestier, who was nearly running by this time, also turned the corner some ten seconds after them.

There was no one in sight.

The corner building, to which the policeman was unashamedly clinging, was the St. Denis-sur-Aisne branch of the Bank of France. The principal entrance was in the main street behind him; down this side street there were four heavily barred windows ten feet from the ground and the small side door which led to the manager's private residence. It was flush with the wall and presented not an inch of cover. Even where the building came to an end the wall of the manager's garden, ten feet high with broken glass on the top, ran on for another twenty yards to connect with the blank wall of a warehouse.

On the opposite side of the road there were the closed doors and windows of the village school and the high wall of its playground, all bathed in the cloudless moonlight of a glorious September night.

"I am ill," said Boulestier despairingly. "I have a fever. I am probably dying."

He turned back into the main road on his way home. A little way past the side turning was André's garage with the Rolls-Bentley inside awaiting attention. When Boulestier reached the garage he glanced in and saw a light in André's little office at the back. The two men were friends, although the *garagiste* was thirty years younger than the policeman. Their duties often kept them up when the rest of the citizens were abed and asleep, and Boulestier had contracted the habit of dropping into the garage on cold nights if André were about. There was an electric fire in the little office and usually a bottle of wine in the cupboard. Boulestier tapped upon the garage doors and André came out to admit him.

"You do not look well," said André. "Your face is white and you are trembling. Has anything happened—are you ill? Come in and rest yourself."

"I am indeed ill," said Boulestier. "I have a fever. I have migraine. My eyes deceive me." He staggered into the office, sat down heavily, and took his head in both hands. "I suffer from delusions." He groaned.

"Let me get the doctor," said André, really alarmed. "Let me summon your wife. Let me—"

"No, no, for heaven's sake not my wife!"

"*Mon Dieu,* what have you been doing?"

"Nothing, nothing. At least, nothing that I ought not. It is what I have just seen."

André laid a hand upon his shoulder, bent over him, and suddenly broke into a laugh.

"You have been drinking, that is all! No wonder your eyes deceive you. Then you come along here and see my little light. 'There is André,' you say, 'my good friend André with a bottle in his cupboard.' So you come in and tell me a sad story. My friend, there is no need; if you want a little something on your way home you shall have it, why not?" He opened his cupboard and took out two glasses and a bottle of Beaujolais. "There you are, drink that and cheer up. *Sante!*"

The policeman emptied the glass at a draught and sighed. "That is better, but indeed I was not making up a story. Listen."

He told his tale with such convincing detail that even André was shaken. "Queer," he said, "very queer, but there must be some rational explanation. Probably you were right, you dreamed the first part, and as for the two men who came from the shop door later, no doubt they were guests of Vigneron's and he let them out himself."

"I should like to think so, but why did I not hear voices when they said *adieu?* Why did I not hear the door shut behind them?"

"They were being very quiet, not to disturb the neighbors."

"It is not like Vigneron, that. Still, it could be. But where did they go when they rounded the corner? If they had been there I must have seen them."

André had his own opinion why Boulestier had not seen them, but he did not put it into words.

"I myself had an odd experience today," he said. "That great and beautiful auto here—you passed it as you came in. Such a car! Yet it broke down by the Englishmen's Barn on the Sedan road this evening and I could find nothing wrong So I must get up before six and work upon it, for it is wanted again by nine." He got up and went to the office door. "Come and look at it, it will do your eyes good. A Rolls-Bentley, no less." He switched on the workshop lights to show the great car gleaming upon the oily concrete floor. "Four—no, five million francs that car is worth; the owner must be a millionaire. They are staying at the Commerce."

He wandered across to the car and Boulestier strolled after him. "You see," said André, "what problems I have to solve. There is nothing the matter so far as I can see, and yet when I switch on nothing happens. See?" He pressed the starter and the engine immediately sprang to life and purred as only a six-cylinder Rolls-Bentley can purr.

André uttered a surprised noise and sat in the car, listening to the engine with his head cocked like a terrier.

"But it goes well," said Boulestier. "Or so it appears to me."

"I shall take her out for a little run. Are you coming? It will do your migraine good, the fresh night air. It is a lovely night and it is not every day that one has a drive in such a car as this."

"For me to push behind, at my age?"

"There will be no need, I think. I will open the garage doors. Will you go out and signal to me if anything comes?"

The great car slid quietly out into the road. Boulestier got in and they moved off into the dappled moonlight.

* * * *

Jeremy and Sally Latimer were sitting in the lounge of the Hôtel duCommerce, Jeremy upon a high stool at the bar with a glass of cognac at his elbow and Sally in a deep armchair nearby listening with fascinated attention while the proprietor—an impassioned and inspired chef—explained how one grills. Electric grills—impossible! Gas grills—barbaric! One grills, naturally, upon charcoal; clear, glowing *charbon-de-bois* the color of a sunset by Titian—

The outer door of the hotel opened; two travelers came into the entrance hall and glanced into the lounge. The proprietor excused himself and went to meet them. They were carrying new and expensive-looking suitcases.

"Good evening," said the elder with a strong English accent. "Could you accommodate us for the night? One room with two beds in it would do."

The proprietor said that he would be charmed. They could have a room each or one with two beds if preferred, as they wished.

"I think," said the younger traveler, "that we will have the one room. We are used to sleeping together."

"But, certainly," said the proprietor, taking their suitcases from them. "Would you care to see your room at once, or would you wish for a little drink first, having come off a journey."

"A little drink would go down very well," said the elder. "It is a very long time since we had a drink."

"Many, many years," said the younger. "Eh, James?"

The proprietor wondered whether this was a joke or whether the two had just been released from jail. They did not look in the least like jailbirds, it must be a joke. He laughed appreciatively.

"No doubt it seems so, messieurs. Be pleased to come this way." He put down their suitcases and took them into the lounge, where, at the sight of Sally, they both bowed much more deeply than is now customary and said that they hoped they did not intrude. Sally bent her head and Jeremy said, "Not at all, welcome," in a bluff, hearty voice.

The proprietor discussed wines with them and went to fetch their order. They were sitting at a small table near the door and looking about them with bright interested eyes, not speaking much and then in low tones. The proprietor came back with glasses on a tray and asked for their opinion of the port. They sipped it and nodded.

"A very sound wine, in my opinion," said the younger. "What say you, James?"

"A little sweet for my taste," said James, "but it is good, as you say, Charles."

"Monsieur is English?" said the proprietor, addressing James, who nodded. "And you, monsieur," turning to Charles, "are from the South of France, are you not?"

"Oh no, you are very far out. I have never been in the South of France; I learned my French in New Orleans."

"In New Orleans," said Jeremy, lifting his glass to them and speaking in English. "Well, now, just fancy that. I come from old Virginia."

"Sir," said Charles, raising his glass, "I am right glad to greet a brother American. But your lovely lady is not one of us.

"Why, no, she's English, but she's made up for that by having the good taste to marry an American. My wife's people come from Lancashire.

"There are some very good old families in Lancashire," said James. "Ma'am, let us join forces and refuse to be patronized by these damned Colonists."

Jeremy stared for a moment and then burst into a roar of laughter.

"Will you listen to that, Sally? Well, well, what's a hundred and seventy years to an Englishman?"

"Tell me," said Sally, leaning forward and addressing Charles, "how did you know I was not American? I don't think I have spoken since you came in."

Charles bit his lip for a moment and then said: "Why, that is just it, ma'am. No American woman would have sat so quiet for so long as you."

"She's not always so quiet," laughed Jeremy. "She's just showing off in company."

" 'My gracious silence,' " quoted James, and Charles looked at him. "Where does that come from?"

"Shakespeare. *Coriolanus.* "

"Now you're showing off. My cousin," added Charles, "is always trying to convince me that Americans are comparatively uneducated. Compared with him, he means."

"Let me make my peace," said James, "by asking you, sir, to do us the honor of drinking with us. Your charming wife may not wish to take alcoholic liquor, but perhaps there is a *sirop* of some sort which she likes, or a cup of coffee?"

Sally laughed. "My wife," said Jeremy, "though not much of a drinker, likes a small glass of something now and then."

"Ma'am, in that case, please——"

"A Cointreau, thank you very much," said Sally.

"And you, sir; I do not know what sort of a cellar is kept here in these days, but I do remember many years ago drinking a very fine brandy here. Also, this port is passable."

Jeremy said he would like brandy, please.

"And you, Charles?"

"What I should really prefer," said Charles wistfully, "is a nice long mint julep in a tall glass."

"I'm afraid you won't find that here," said Jeremy, "though they will do you one in Paris if you go to the right place."

"I shall ask you, sir, to favor me with the address of that blessed spot."

"Harry's New York Bar in the Rue Daunou for a start," said Jeremy. "We'll get together and I'll make out a little tour of Paris for you. But I gather that you gentlemen have been here before?"

"Many years ago," said James. He signaled to the proprietor and gave him the order.

"Between the wars, I suppose," continued Jeremy, "since you gentlemen are certainly not old enough to have fought in World War One and it isn't all that long since 1945." The two men looked at him with expressions so completely blank that he naturally assumed that they had not heard what he said. "It would be between the wars," he repeated.

Charles looked at James, who gave a sudden barking laugh. "I would have said that it was precisely in the midst of one," he said.

The proprietor came back with a tray of glasses and handed them round and said something to James in a low tone. He looked as though the remark had startled him and turned to Charles.

"Have you any money with you, Cousin?"

"Er—not enough. In our suitcases we have plenty."

James rose to his feet, merely sipped his brandy with a polite bow to the young Latimers, and set it down again. "I must ask you to excuse us for a few moments. Landlord, if we might go up to our room with our luggage? We had an unfortunate experience with pickpockets once," he explained, "so we only carry a few francs with us. The rest travels in our valises." He went out, followed by Charles, and the proprietor could be seen leading the way upstairs.

They were led along a twisting passage and shown into a large room which looked out upon a courtyard. The proprietor switched on the electric light by the door as he entered and carried the luggage in. "There are lights over both beds," he said, "and the water is hot in the taps." He set the suitcases upon two chairs and went out of the room.

The room had two beds in it, one double and one single; there were thick curtains with bobble fringes at the window, an elaborate cornice round the ceiling, and a dark green wallpaper with a large pattern on it. The furniture was of heavy mahogany and there was a large mirror in a carved gilt frame on one wall.

"Very nice," said Charles, staring about him. "Quite modern furniture and the latest style of decoration, surprising. But what is that thing on the wall?"

He approached the fixed handbasin and tentatively turned on a tap, but James recalled him sharply.

"We were idiots," he said. "We ought to have remembered that we should want some money. Did you hear what the fellow was asking for those few drinks? Over six hundred francs!"

Charles was pushing the rubber plug into the waste and pulling it out again with a soft pop. "Marvelous," he said. "Extraordinary. Works just like your new bath, James. Yes, money. Did you not notice the prices in that shop? A thousand francs and more for the most inferior shirt which no gentleman would be seen dead in." He laughed.

"It is not a matter for jesting," said James. "Something very peculiar has happened to the French currency, but we cannot go into that now. I completely forgot about money."

Charles abandoned his new toy. "If we want money, Cousin James, we must go where money is. The local bank. We know where that is; it is on the corner round which that foolish policeman pursued us." He crossed the room to stand beside his cousin. "It is simple, it will not take us five minutes." They looked at their reflections in the mirror. "I do not like the cut of this coat, Cousin James, nor of yours; they sit too close to the nape of the neck. Never mind, it is how they are worn in these days. Our cousin Jeremy's fits even closer, I notice. Well, shall we go?"

The room door did not open nor the heavy curtains move by the windows, but the mirror showed only the great double bed and a corner of the mahogany wardrobe.

Ten minutes later they strolled cheerfully down the stairs again and reentered the lounge. James tossed a thousand franc note to the pro-

prietor, who was relieved to see it. It was true that these travelers were
well dressed and had expensive and heavy suitcases, but one never knows
in these days, and any sort of trouble is a thing to be avoided.

"Have you gentlemen come from Paris?" asked Jeremy.

"No. Not from Paris, we are on our way there. And you?"

"Well, we hope to reach Paris tomorrow, but my car picked up a
gremlin just outside this place this evening, and if the local *garagiste*
can't put his finger on the trouble I don't know when we'll get going."

"A—a gremlin?"

"Sorry. You are not conversant with your British Air Force slang?
When some not readily diagnosed trouble occurs in the bus, they say it's
a gremlin, which I gather they visualize as a small imp or demon inter-
fering with the mechanism." James coughed and the corners of Charles's
long mouth curled up irrepressibly. "Of course there's no such thing as
gremlins and they know there's no such thing, it's just their picturesque
way of thinking. They are a fine bunch of lads, your British Air Force,
yes, sir."

The front door of the hotel opened and the *garagiste* André looked
into the lounge. Jeremy sprang to his feet and André said that, as he
had seen lights in the hotel, he thought it just worth while looking in to
see if Monsieur was still about. There was good news. The Rolls-Bentley
was now in perfect order.

"Good," said Jeremy. "Good. Splendid. Come and have a drink. Well,
that is good news. What was the trouble?"

"Simple, monsieur, when one think of it. A little corrosion on the
wiring terminals on the battery," said André, who had had time to compose an explanation.

"But the current was getting through to the plugs—"

"Intermittently, no doubt, monsieur, but not when under load," said
André. "Thank you, just a little glass of red wine. Thank you, your health."
He bowed to Sally and tossed off his wine. "I will bring her round at
nine, if that suits Monsieur? She is all right now, she is outside. I thought
Monsieur would wish me to make sure, so I tried her out. What an auto!
What a dream! I shall always remember having had the privilege of driv-
ing her. I will wish Monsieur and Madame a good night," said André,
backing to the door. "I could not sleep before I had dealt with the trouble.
Good night, the company." He went out and the front door banged
behind him.

"Well, that is good news," said Jeremy. "We'll be away to Paris in the
morning after all, Sally."

"So your gremlin is discovered and defeated?" said Charles, smiling.

"It would seem so, sir. I hope so. The expression amuses you, I don't wonder. By the way, were you thinking of traveling to Paris tomorrow morning? I was about to say that there are two vacant seats in the back of the car. If you two gentlemen would care for a lift to Paris I should be glad to have you.... Not at all, not at all," as Charles tried to thank him. "If we Americans don't back each other up, who will? By the way, the name is Latimer, Jeremy Latimer and his wife Sally."

"Thank you, sir," said Charles. "Thank you indeed. Your suggestion is more than courteous, Mr.—is it Mr.?—Latimer; it is amazing kind of you and we are delighted to accept. Eh, James?"

"Charmed and delighted," said James. "A thousand thanks, Mr. Latimer. By the way, by a very odd coincidence our name is also Latimer. I am James and this is my cousin, Major Charles Latimer."

"Of the American Army, no doubt."

Charles nodded. "Of the South, naturally."

"Well, well, we must talk about that in the morning. It wouldn't surprise me if we turned out to be related, Major Latimer."

"I should not," said Charles, "be at all surprised."

Sally got up. "If we're going off to Paris at squeak of dawn tomorrow I'm off to bed. How much longer are you going to sit up, darling? It's nearly one."

"Not any longer, honey. I'm coming up with you."

They were all on their feet exchanging good nights when the hotel's front door burst open and an agitated woman thrust her head in. The proprietor rushed forward.

"Oh, excuse me, I'm sure, she said. "My husband, is he here?"

"Boulestier? No. I have not seen him at all this evening."

"Oh, where can he be? There is a telephone call from Paris. Excuse me, the company." The head vanished and the door banged again.

"The wife of the policeman," said the proprietor. "She is of those who agitate themselves unnecessarily."

"She looks a bit like a wet hen," said Jeremy. "I hope she finds him. Well, good night, everybody."

"Good night!"

"Good night!"

"Good night—"

CHAPTER IV:
Trouble at the Bank

THE BANK MANAGER, Monsieur Cayeux, was giving a card party to three of his friends: Monsieur Petier, the mayor of St. Denis, Monsieur

Vigneron of the departmental store, and Monsieur Grober, the postmaster. Cayeux lived in a flat over the bank, and the room in which they were sitting was over the strong-room. They were playing bridge of a not too tiresomely scientific kind—"after all, bridge is only a game"— and the stakes were of a modesty befitting a bank manager and a postmaster who wished to remain in office.

"Pass," said the postmaster, who hated having to open the bidding.

"Two clubs," said the mayor.

"Two clubs, eh?" said Vigneron. "Well, well, we must see what we can do when attacked by two clubs. Well, well. I say two hearts. Now then, Cayeux?"

"Pass," said Cayeux. "I will leave it to Grober."

"I cannot bear to disappoint the company," said the postmaster. "Two spades."

"So that is where they all are," said the mayor. "And nobody likes diamonds, do they? Well, now I think——"

"Hush!" said Cayeux suddenly. "Listen!"

"I hear nothing," said Grober after a moment's silence.

"Nor I," said Vigneron. "What did you think you heard, Cayeux?"

"Some noise from downst——Listen!"

"I thought I heard something then," said Petier, the mayor. "What is directly under this room, Cayeux?"

"My strong-room."

"It is nothing," said Vigneron. "It is the wind. What do you bid, Mayor?"

"There is no wind," said Cayeux. "The night is as still—— Hark!"

"Don't keep saying 'Hark!' like that," said the postmaster. "You make me nervous."

"Excuse me for one moment, gentlemen," said Cayeux. "I am sure it is nothing, but I am going down just to set my mind at rest."

"It is a window swinging," said Vigneron, picking up the cards he had laid down. "Petier, you were about to say——"

But the mayor put down his cards and rose to his feet. "I well come with you, Cayeux," he said, "though I am sure it is only the cat."

"The wine is on the side table," said Cayeux, and left the room, followed by Petier.

"I do not think we need disturb ourselves," said Grober. "Let me pour you a glass of wine, Vigneron, since our friend suggested it."

"An excellent idea," said Vigneron. "I must admit I am more interested in wine than in cats."

Cayeux and Petier went down the narrow staircase which led from the manager's flat to his private entrance. At the foot of the stair there was a tiny lobby; the outer door faced them and on the right was another door leading into the bank.

Cayeux unlocked it and switched on the light inside the room.

He heard a grunt from the mayor and was in the act of turning when he found himself seized from behind and a large hand closed over his mouth. He did his best to bite it, but artificial teeth are not effective as weapons of offense and he was nearly choked by them. He had barely pushed them back into position when he was capably gagged with what tasted like a woolen stocking; he was then pushed down on the only chair the room contained and tied to it. When his head cleared enough to let him look round he saw Petier, the mayor, similarly gagged and bound, lying on the floor trying to kick a second villain, who was lashing his ankles together. There were two men and they wore masks over the lower part of their faces. One of them addressed Cayeux.

"So good of you, Monsieur the Bank Manager, to come downstairs. It saves us the trouble of picking your locks."

"He has the keys, then?" said the other.

"He had; I have them now." He held up the keys of the strong-room door and the bank safe. "Of course he had them, bank managers wear their keys even in bed. By the way, lock that door we came in at, which Monsieur so politely opened for us. He left the key in the lock outside."

The second man took the key from outside the door, which he shut and locked.

The room they were in was merely an anteroom to the strong-room and contained only a small table, one chair, and a carpet on the floor. The strong-room itself was entered through a heavy iron door opening outwards and had two walls covered with the small locked cupboards which are the safe-deposits. In the farthest corner was the bank safe, very large and solid, and in the middle of the room another table for the convenience of those who wished to look over their valuables. The procedure when a bank customer wished to open his safe-deposit was for one of the clerks to admit him to the strong-room, lock him in, and then sit on the chair in the anteroom until the customer was ready to come out again.

The robbers left Cayeux tied to his chair and went to the strong-room door with his keys. There was an electric-light switch outside the door which they switched on without apparent effect, but when the door was opened the inner room was seen to be lighted. The first man entered, leaving Cayeux's key in the lock; the second man followed him in. The heavy door swung to but did not quite lock.

Cayeux in his chair was only a couple of yards from the door. His feet were on the floor although tied to the front legs of the chair; he managed to lean forward until the chair came off the floor and then waddled painfully, an inch at a time, bearing as it were his house on his back like a snail, until he reached the strong-room door. He threw himself against it, and the heavy door closed with a satisfying click.

"Aaagh!" said Cayeux through his gag, and tottered wildly in the attempt to keep his balance. At the cost of banging his head painfully upon the door, he succeeded. The mayor, grunting with effort, rolled across the floor towards him but could not help him.

Cayeux rested, gasping, since a gag impedes breathing, and then rose to his feet again. He appeared to be rubbing his face on the door, and Petier thought he had gone mad and was trying to bite it, then he saw that Cayeux was attempting to scrape off his gag upon the projecting key.

Suddenly, from within the strong-room there came the sounds of conflict. Cries of anger, thuds as of blows, and a sound of splintering wood. Grober and Vigneron, peacefully discussing politics in the room overhead, heard it and rushed downstairs, only to be stopped by the locked door of the anteroom. They were not men of violence and had never broken open a locked door in all their blameless lives. They hammered upon the panels and shouted: "Open! Open!" The mayor, still overheating himself with fruitless effort upon the floor, turned purple with anger; Cayeux, still mortifying his features against the key, ground his teeth. At long last the gag came off his mouth and immediately his cries filled the quiet night.

"Help! Help! Robbers! Assassins! Get the police! Help! Grober, Vigneron, call the police! One robs the bank! Help!"

Effective help was at hand. André and Boulestier, driving back to the garage from the Hôtel du Commerce—where the policeman had modestly waited outside—were passing the bank at the moment when the cries broke forth. The Rolls-Bentley stopped and they leapt out, Boulestier drawing his large revolver and André snatching up a heavy spanner. They reached the manager's private door at the moment when Vigneron opened it with a full-throated yell of "Police!"

"Here," said Boulestier from six inches away, and Vigneron fell back. "One calls 'Police,' " continued Boulestier, majestically advancing, "and here I am. Show me your robbers."

"In—in there. But the door remains locked."

"Help! Police!" urged Cayeux's voice from within.

"Coming! Break me down this door," said Boulestier to André.

"I'll just get a——" said André, running towards his garage so fast that the word "hammer" floated back to them like an echo. Almost before the sound of his footsteps had ceased they were heard again, returning, and André arrived.

"What," said Vigneron, retiring backwards up the stair, "is that thing?"

"Two-handed flogging hammer," said André. "Stand clear, the company."

They scattered as he lined up the lock on the door and shifted into the right position. The hammer had a ten-pound head on a four-foot shaft; André swung it back round his shoulder and brought it down directly upon the keyhole. The door flew open.

They all rushed into the room and delivered the mayor and the bank manager from bondage.

"Where are the robbers?" asked Boulestier.

"In the strong-room, locked in," said Cayeux indistinctly, for he was dabbing his mouth, which was bleeding.

"They are quiet enough now," said the mayor. "They were fighting in there a few minutes ago."

"Fighting?" said André incredulously. "In there?"

"Over their ill-gotten gains, no doubt," said Vigneron.

"Well, that's a damn silly place to fight," said André.

"Stand back," said Boulestier, who had been, as it were, winding himself up to start. "André, with me. Monsieur Cayeux, open me the door, if you please."

Cayeux turned the key and pulled the heavy door towards him; as soon as it was sufficiently wide open Boulestier, revolver in hand, marched in with André at his heels while the others stood on tiptoe, craning their necks to see what was within.

One man was lying on the floor beneath one of the safe-deposits, which was standing open; the other was sprawled on his face before the safe, also wide open. The small table was upset and a light chair, kept there for the convenience of customers, was smashed in pieces. Bundles of notes from the safe were lying about the floor.

"Are—are they dead?" quavered Vigneron.

"Not in the least dead," said Boulestier. One of the men was beginning to stir and Boulestier handcuffed his wrists behind his back. "Some of that cord, if you please," he said, and the second man was similarly secured with that which had impeded Cayeux in the execution of his duty. "One does not expect to require more than one pair of handcuffs in the course of the evening. Now let us move them into the anteroom."

They were dragged out with trailing heels and dumped in the anteroom while Cayeux made what he called "a hasty checkup." The bundles of notes which were upon the floor were all of large denominations, the equivalent of five- and ten-pound notes, and these appeared to be complete, but the bank manager said that some hundred thousand francs in small notes was missing—about a hundred pounds sterling.

"It is simple," said the mayor. "The money is in their pockets."

But it was not. There was money in their pockets, naturally, about five pounds in one case and seven or eight in the other, but nothing resembling one hundred pounds anywhere upon their persons. One of them was reasonably conscious by this time and the justly enraged Cayeux rushed at him and kicked him in the ribs.

"Villain! Scoundrel! What have you done with my money?"

"Never touched your money."

"Rat! Weasel! You lie."

"This one," said Boulestier, with the air of one who must be just if it kills him, "was, in effect, the one by the safe-deposit, It was the other jailbird who was near the safe."

"He must speak," said Cayeux desperately. "Beat him. He shall speak."

The other jailbird looked as though he were still unconscious, but when André picked him up and shook him as a housewife shakes a mat—André was six feet tall and immensely strong—the man revived suspiciously quickly.

"Money," said André. "Where is it? Speak, or I will shake you till your eyes drop out."

"I haven't got it. I haven't got it. I never had it—"

André shook him.

"Mercy—mercy! I tell you, I opened the safe with the key and went to tell Michel here that I had done so, and the fool turned round and hit me."

"You hit me first," said Michel. "You came up behind without a word and struck me upon the ear. Look, gentlemen—"

It was quite evident that the ear had, indeed, been recently hit.

"I turned round," pursued Michel, "and there was Gaston here staggering upon his feet with a face like the devil in person. I thought he had gone mad—"

"It is you who went mad. You struck me upon the mouth—"

That, also, was obviously true.

"While I was disabled by your first coward's blow—"

"Coward? Call me a—"

"I call you a—!"

"You picked up the chair and smashed it upon my head and shoulders——

"You threw the table at me—"

"Liar! Cheat!"

"Double-crossing blackguard—"

"Stop that!" thundered Boulestier. "Order in court! Not that this is actually a court, but I will have order!"

"But where is the money?" demanded Cayeux.

"Now I come to think of it," said Gaston in suddenly quiet tones, "I remember distinctly knocking out Michel and seeing him crash to the floor, and after that the table came at me and hit me on the head."

"The *table* hit you?" said the mayor. "The table? Are you seriously asserting that the table, of its own volition, raised itself from the floor, propelled itself through the air, and struck itself upon your head?"

"Yes," said Gaston stubbornly. "That is what happened, although," he added modestly, "I hardly expect to be believed."

"In the course of thirty-four years and seven months in the police force," said Boulestier, "that is quite the silliest story I have ever heard."

"But the money," wailed Cayeux.

"There is also the safe-deposit," said Grober, the postmaster. "Is there anything missing from that? Whose is it?"

"That," said Cayeux sternly, "is confidential." He went across to the safe-deposit; the door was hanging open and the contents, typewritten sheets folded up and envelopes with rubber bands round them, were lying together upon the floor where Michel had let them fall. "In any case, I shall have to refer to my records"—he picked up a packet of envelopes to look at the addresses on them—"before I can be quite certain . . ." His voice died away. The interested watchers on the threshold saw that he had flushed scarlet and was biting his lip. After a quick examination he gathered up, with desperate haste, the papers lying on the floor and stuffed them back into the compartment. He was about to slam the door and lock it when Boulestier stopped him.

"Halt. You must not touch that."

"Touch what?"

"The key. It must be fingerprinted and produced in evidence in court. Probably the little door will have to be taken off its hinges and produced also." Boulestier advanced into the strong-room. "You must leave it as it is until the experts have been here. Come away! What are you—"

Cayeux whirled round and backed against the safe-deposit; his face was now quite pale, but his eyes were shining and he was plainly determined not to give way.

"Cayeux," said the mayor, "come away. You are overwrought, it is understandable, you are unstrung. It is the reaction, nobody blames you. Come upstairs and lie down; what you need is a little cognac and some aspirin. Come, Cayeux, come, the papers will be quite safe there."

"No, no, you do not understand—"

"Let me suggest," said André. "I have here a small pair of pliers. If I push the door shut with them and very carefully turn the key with them, it will not damage the fingerprints and the contents will be safe, *hein?*"

It was done. Cayeux simmered down and allowed himself to be led out of the strong-room, still asking an unresponsive Providence to tell him where the money was. Boulestier was in the act of arranging with André to help him conduct the prisoners to the cells, when there came a tapping at the outer door, and there was Madame Boulestier.

"Jules—at last! I have been raking the village for you. There is Paris on the telephone; they have heard that two dangerous bank robbers are coming to break in here and you must watch for them—there are descriptions—you must come and speak to them at once, they are holding the line—come!"

"Return, woman," said Jules, speaking as from a great height, "return and tell Paris I have arrested the criminals and am now conveying them to custody. Don't stand there gaping, go! André, with me. Come on, the prisoners."

Grober, the postmaster, and Vigneron, the shopkeeper, walked back along the moonlit street together.

"But what I want to know," said Vigneron, "is what the devil did Cayeux find in that cupboard?"

"I knew there was something," said Cayeux, suddenly sitting up in bed in the dark. "Why did I hear a noise in the strong-room *before* those men went in?"

CHAPTER V
Bells of Shandon

THE BANK ROBBERS were men whom the Paris police had long desired to catch; they were both in that tiresome category of persons whom the police know, but cannot prove, to be guilty. They were not ill-dressed thugs from the slums; they were well-spoken, looked like unimportant businessmen, and lived in neat villas at Passy. When, therefore, they had been captured red-handed by Constable Jules Boulestier at St. Denis-sur-Aisne, the Sûreté in Paris promptly sent one of their best men there to look over the evidence and make sure that there was no slip this time.

He interviewed Boulestier and congratulated him on his capture, told him he would be a sergeant in a month's time with effect from the date of the burglary, and heard his story. It did not include any reference to the queer apparition of the two naked men because Boulestier had convinced himself that that was a dream. He had been sitting on the bench when he first thought he saw them and he was still sitting there when he woke up. One does not report dreams to one's superior officers in any case, and particularly not when it involves having been asleep on duty.

The Sûreté man was delighted with Boulestier's story and went on to interview Cayeux, who showed him the scene of the crime and also the contents of the safe-deposit. At this point the look of delight faded slowly from the detective's face and an expression of profound thought took its place.

"The key of this safe-deposit," he began.

"Was in the lock," said Cayeux. "Constable Boulestier took it away for fingerprinting. Those men must have brought it with them."

"Without doubt," said the detective. "But you have a duplicate, since you have just opened it for me."

"Certainly," agreed the bank manager. "A necessary precaution in case a customer should lose his key."

"Certainly," said the detective. "Undoubtedly." He relapsed into such profound thought that Cayeux became nervous.

"All banks do that," he said timidly. "It is the rule."

"Yes, I know," said the detective absently. He thought for a moment longer and seemed to make up his mind, for he patted Cayeux upon the shoulder and said that that would be all for the moment. "You will have to give evidence at the trial, of course, but as regards all this stuff"— he tapped the door of the safe-deposit with his finger— "silence, my friend, silence!"

"My dear sir," protested Cayeux, "do you suppose I have worked in a bank for thirty years without learning to hold my tongue?"

"Of course not, but sometimes the temptation is greater than at other times, is it not?"

The two men looked each other in the eyes and appeared to understand each other. Cayeux smiled faintly and stood back to let the Sûreté man precede him from the strong-room.

The detective went to Vonziers to interview the examining magistrate who would conduct the preliminary enquiry.

"This case of these two rascals who broke into the bank at St. Denis," he said. "We shall have to be very, very careful. It turns out to be a political matter."

"Political!" said the magistrate, and his stiff white eyebrows went up.

"Yes." The detective hesitated. "The matter is so delicate that I hardly like to mention names even to you."

"I would rather you did not; then, if anyone asks me, I can truthfully say that you did not tell me."

The detective nodded. "There is a certain Minister, a brilliantly clever man. Yet there hangs about his name a sort of miasma of dubiety."

"In the present state of politics," said the magistrate acidly, "that remark would not serve to identify any one man."

"Some people call him the Caterpillar," said the detective cautiously.

"Oh, him! Really!"

"The safe-deposit contained more than a dozen letters written to him and a duplicate typescript of an agreement and a list of names."

"Idiot," said the magistrate. "Why did he not burn them?"

"I presume he thought they might come in usefully at some time. The safe-deposit was not, of course, in his own name. However, the point is this. Those two beauties now in custody did not break into the bank for money. They came, provided with the safe-deposit key, to get those papers."

"I begin to see," said the magistrate. "His political opponents sent them, of course. If we were not, on account of our office, politically impartial, I should say that it was a smart bit of work. Eh?"

The detective smiled slowly. "The members of that card party were the bank manager, the mayor, the postmaster, and the principal store-keeper."

"The leading citizens, in fact."

"And they are all members of the political party opposed to the Caterpillar."

The magistrate sat up.

"And the bank manager," finished the detective, "has, naturally, duplicate keys to the safe-deposits. But the important point is," he went on, forestalling the magistrate, who was about to speak, "that no word of all this should leak out. It would be a political scandal of the first order and we have too many political scandals already. This one would shake France to the foundations."

"But can nothing be done to this—this traitor?"

"I rang up Paris before I left St. Denis, but the fellow must have second sight. He left France by air this morning and I do not suppose that he will ever come back. So long as he never returns I do not care where he goes. Our object is secured, is it not?"

"I would rather he were dead," said the magistrate thoughtfully, "but one cannot have everything in this life. Well, now, about these robbers of yours?"

"My department suggests that they be charged with breaking and entering the bank and feloniously assaulting the bank manager and the mayor. Not a word about stealing or attempting to steal or opening a safe-deposit or being in unlawful possession of a safe-deposit key without the owner's authority."

"I see. But if they were—to be blunt—all in it together, why assault the bank manager? To say nothing of the mayor?"

"They did not appear to me to have been very painfully assaulted," said the detective dryly.

"Oh, ah. I see. No black eyes, no gory noses, eh? Well, now, there is a little item here about a hundred thousand francs in small notes, what do we do about that?"

"Speaking as one good citizen to another, I should say it was cheap at the price."

The magistrate laughed aloud. "You think the manager borrowed it for a temporary emergency?"

"And will presently find it had been put away in the wrong place," nodded the detective. "He had to report it, of course, or his chief cashier would have noticed it."

"I think that all fits in very well indeed," said the examining magistrate.

It was not until two days later that the sub-manager in charge of the Gentlemen's Outfitting Department of Messrs. Aristide Vigneron et Cie. reported missing two complete suits of lightweight cloth of a superior quality. There were dozens of suits hanging close-packed upon racks under glass and it was impossible to tell exactly how long they had been missing since they came in three months earlier. Enquiries were made but nothing came of it, and the fact that a small but adequate selection of vests, pants, socks, and ties was also missing was not discovered for months. The Luggage, Garden, Implements, and Ironmongery Departments reported two good suitcases gone, but this was put down to shoplifting and so were two hats. These were rather wider in the brim than was popular at the moment and had been in stock some time; Vigneron not distress himself much about them.

He had all his floor managers into his office and scolded them roundly for carelessness and inattention to duty, fined the unfortunate losers of the suits and the suitcases, and threatened terrible reprisals if such a thing ever happened again.

Sergeant Boulestier heard the sad story but, as he did not receive an official complaint, he naturally said nothing. One does not serve in the police force for thirty-four years and seven months without learning tact.

Jeremy Latimer and his wife left St. Denis-sur-Aisne for Paris soon after ten in the morning after the raid on the bank. Sally sat in the front seat beside her husband; in the incredibly comfortable rear seats of the Rolls-Bentley were Charles and James Latimer, their good suitcases at their feet and their rather too wide-brimmed hats firmly on their heads. Jeremy drove slowly until they were clear of the little town and then, upon a particularly good stretch of the Route Nationale, put his foot down. The speedometer needle rose past sixty to seventy, then eighty, and finally settled, quivering like a butterfly, upon the eighty-five mark and steadied there.

"Charles!" muttered James, gripping the armrests till his knuckles turned white. "Charles! What is happening?"

"We are traveling, Cousin James, that is all." Charles also was clinging to the armrest, but his eyes were shining and his voice was exultant. "By Gad, sir, this is marvellous! It is like flying!"

"It is excessively dangerous," said James severely. "It— there is something coming—we shall all be killed!"

Charles burst out laughing. "Oh no, we shall not, you forget. Whatever may happen to anyone else in this world, we shall be none the worse."

James relaxed at once and turned to his cousin. "By Jove, Charles, you are in the right. I had forgotten. How strange, how exquisite, to be able to indulge the maddest whim with no fear of the consequences." He laughed suddenly, that odd barking laugh of his. "By Gad, Charles, I feel as though I had never lived before."

Sally heard them laughing and turned round. "We're not going too fast for you, are we?"

"No, no," said James. "You cannot go too fast for us. If men ever fly through the air, it will feel like this."

Sally naturally thought that she had misheard what he said. "Haven't you ever flown, then?"

"Oh no," said James simply. "Dear me, no. Things are not like that with us at all."

Charles kicked him heavily on the ankle and James blushed and subsided into his corner.

"How fast," asked Charles, "will this—this vehicle go?"

"I have got a hundred and twenty out of her," said Jeremy, speaking over his shoulder, "on a real good stretch of the Great North Road between Doncaster and Newark, but there aren't many places where a man can really let his car out over this side. You wait, Sally, till we get to the States where a highway is a highway and not cluttered up with little towns every few hundred yards."

Far in the distance towards Paris there appeared a speck in the sky, growing rapidly larger. James was the first to notice it; he jogged Charles's elbow.

"Look," he murmured. "What is that marvel?"

"Someone has really invented a machine that will fly—ah! I have it. That was what our young lady cousin meant just now when she asked if we had ever flown."

"She's your cousin," corrected James, "but she's my great grand-daughter. Yes, no doubt, but how vast a machine it is. How does it stay up without any balloons attached to it?"

"There are no balloons," said Charles. He leaned forward to speak to Jeremy. "Can you tell me what that machine is, if you please?"

Jeremy glanced up. "Paris to Amsterdam, KLM air liner, I expect, or Sabena. That'll be the one we went up on last year, honey." He looked at the dashboard clock. "That's right. She'll be in Amsterdam at eleven o'clock."

"Thank you, sir," said Charles rather faintly. "Most interesting, most."

They came into Rheims and stopped for coffee in the square out-side the great west front of the cathedral. The elder Latimers sprang out of the car as soon as it stopped and hurried round to Sally's door. James opened it and held it while Charles, bowing, offered his arm to help Sally to alight. She laid two fingers upon it and stepped out with a laughing word of thanks while Jeremy frankly stared, for it was plain that the two older men were quite naturally performing an ordinary act of courtesy. They followed her, side by side, with their hats in their hands, while she led the way to a table, then one drew out a chair for her while the other pulled back the table and carefully replaced it when she had seated herself. They bowed again and said: "With your permission?" before they sat down themselves. Jeremy, who was not wearing a hat, lounged after them, rubbing his jaw thoughtfully as though he were afraid of its coming loose.

When they had given their order, Jeremy handed round cigarettes, rather gingerly handled by his passengers, pulled up his trousers at the knees, and leaned forward.

"I was most interested last night, Mr. Latimer," he began, address-ing Charles, "to hear you say that your name was Latimer like mine and that you came from Virginia. I believe you said you came from Virginia?"

"I cannot be perfectly assured whether I said so last night or not, but I certainly do," said Charles. "Yes, sir, I am a Virginian born and bred."

"In that case, it would seem as though we ought to be some sort of relations," went on Jeremy. "My father is Henry Latimer, a lawyer in Richmond, Virginia. That is, his office is in the town but he has a little place just outside where my sister Louella and I were born. My mother's name was Jefferson."

"An honored name," said Charles reverently. "Yes, sir, an honored and distinguished name."

There was a short and rather awkward pause.

"And you, sir?" said Jeremy.

"I come from Shandon," said Charles dreamily. "Yes, sir, Shandon in Virginia is my home town. We had a place about five miles out; I and my brothers were constantly in the habit of riding into town to collect the mail and order such things as were needed on the estate. Also"—he laughed apologetically—"to show off ourselves and our horses before the windows of the parsonage. Parson Beckett's daughter was the loveliest girl I ever saw anywhere until, ma'am, I had the great privilege of meeting you. All the young men of the district were aspirants for the hand of beautiful Rose Beckett."

"And were you successful, Mr. Latimer?" asked Sally.

"I? No. I am a bachelor, ma'am. She married my brother Henry and they were very happy until the war came. I came to Europe and I have not been back since."

"I know Shandon well," said Jeremy. "I've stayed there with friends, but I never heard that there were any Latimers there now. My great-grandfather lived at Shandon until the Civil War, then the house was wrecked and the estate ruined and he moved to Richmond. Sir, we must be cousins. What is your first name?"

"Charles."

"I have no cousins of that name so far as I know. There was one Charles Latimer who was, I believe, my great-grandfather's brother. One of them; I think there were five sons and they all fought in the Civil War. This Charles was a bit of a lad by all accounts——"

"Excuse me—a what?" The corners of Charles's mouth persisted in curling up and his dark eyes were full of laughter.

"Bit of a lad—rather wild. Loved horses and had an eye for the ladies and all that."

James laughed aloud. "He seems to have made something of a mark upon his generation if his reputation has lasted until now. What became of this interesting scamp?"

"He came over to England after the war——"

"And came to my family," said Sally. "I am a Latimer, too, by birth as well as marriage; Jeremy and I are distant cousins. There's a portrait of this Charles Latimer in the old house at home. Lots of whiskers and a gray uniform."

"Nearly all whiskers," said Jeremy, "lovely curly ones. Sir, his eyes and nose are lost in the shrubbery."

Charles ran a thoughtful hand round his clean-shaven jaw and pulled at his mustache.

I recollect it perfectly." He pointed to double doors which still had a delicate fanlight tracery above them, but the doors were crossed by iron bars padlocked together. There was an inscription painted on them: *Magazin de R. Poitevin et Cie., Ameublements.*

"Well, it's a furniture store now, cousins an' gentlemen," said Jeremy. "What in hell is the matter with those cats?"

Three cats had arrived mysteriously from no ascertainable source, two black and one tabby, and were revolving round James and Charles Latimer, tails erect, whiskers quivering, and broad smiles upon their faces.

"I have no idea," said James with some embarrassment. "Go away!"

"These other doors," said Charles, "have brass plates upon them. 'M. Eduard DuPont, Agent. MM. Vallon et Coutel, Importers.' Damn you, sir," to the tabby, "get away!"

The tabby dodged his foot, ran up his back, and stood upon his shoulder, only to leap off the next moment with a yell of terror, and all three cats fled.

"Come on," said Jeremy, "let's get out of here. This place gives me the willies. What did you do to drive off those cats?"

"Nothing, Cousin," said Charles blandly, "nothing whatever, believe me," but his wide mouth curled up at the corners and it was plain that he was suppressing a laugh. Jeremy looked at him doubtfully and turned to lead the way out, with Charles and James following after. James turned, smiling widely, to Charles, who murmured so that Jeremy could not hear.

"You could not expect the faithful Ulysses to put up with that, could you?"

"So long as no one else sees him," answered James.

"Maybe your hotel has moved someplace else," said Jeremy. "I'll ask somebody." There was a small *bistro* next to the archway, in the street, and he went in there while his cousins stood by the car and waited, looking round them. Five minutes later he returned, looking puzzled.

"There's an old girl in there who says she can just remember the hotel being open when she was a child and then it was shut up. It hasn't been a hotel, she says, for more than fifty years."

There was a pause which would soon have become awkward if James had not been quick to break it.

"Nonsense," he said, "nonsense. The old crone is in her dotage. We stayed there just before the war."

"We were still there when war broke out," said Charles.

"Well, that settles it," said Jeremy. "She's bats and I was the mug. O.K., O.K., I often am. Well, now, where do we go from here?"

"I suggest we go back to your hotel, Cousin Jeremy. Your charming lady looks tired. We can alight there and take a *fiacre* to find accommodation; the driver will have some suggestions to make, no doubt."

They drove back to the Ambassador, where the Rolls-Bentley received the notice it deserved. The elder Latimers put their suitcases down on the edge of the pavement and completed their graceful farewells. "When we have found accommodation we will apprise you by messenger," said James.

"That's right," said Jeremy heartily. "Ring us up. You'll get a taxi all right, won't you? See you some more. Come on, Sally——"

He was interrupted by a gleeful cry from Charles. "There is a *fiacre! Cocher! Cocher!*"

The one-horse open Victoria is still occasionally seen upon the streets of Paris, and one of them was passing at the moment. The driver drew in to the curb in response to the Latimer yells and spacious gestures and the cousins climbed happily aboard.

"Come on, Sally," said Jeremy, taking his wife by the arm. "Cousin James was right, you do look tired."

"I feel tired, and you look it, too, darling."

"I am, a bit. Don't ask me why, since we've only driven a hundred and fifty miles, for I wouldn't know."

"I do, though," said Sally, noticing the great clock. "It's past two and we want our lunch, that's all."

Coffee and cigarettes in the Ambassador lounge after lunch. Sally stretched luxuriously and smiled at Jeremy.

"I'm feeling better, aren't you?"

"I sure am. It's a very, very queer thing how an empty stomach will put ideas into your head."

"Perhaps that's why the early saints fasted."

"Now, what is all this about early saints? I was getting all sorts of funny ideas about our new cousins, but now I come to think it over there's nothing to it."

"They are a queer pair," said Sally.

"They are a pair of jokers, that's what. They are putting on an act and, boy, can they act! They must have read it all up someplace. It's a good act, too, I'll say it'll go over big."

"But why? I mean, why do they do it?"

"Well, why not? Guess we all do some little thing to amuse folks, don't we? Look at all the guys who go round telling funny stories all day long, and do they work hard for their laughs, some of 'em! Our cousins have thought up a new hokum, and is it good or is it? I bet they're over here on a vacation and they're just letting themselves go. I just love to see them walking around after you, hat in hand, as though you were royalty. It's a new one on me, wish I'd thought of it myself."

"They have lovely manners," said Sally. "Do you think they really are our cousins?"

"I wouldn't know, but I'll tell you this. They wrote their names in the register at the Hôtel du Commerce at St. Denis before they knew who we were, and the name they wrote was Latimer. I saw it in the morning when the proprietor reminded me I hadn't registered overnight."

"So they wrote theirs first. It does look as though their name really is Latimer, but it doesn't prove that they are cousins of ours."

"Of course not," said Jeremy, "but I just hope they are. I like those guys."

"So do I. I think they're sweet. Oh, darling, I've just remembered something about the original Charles Latimer, the one who came over after the Civil War. He had a pet monkey he used to take about with him everywhere and he called it Ulysses after General Grant."

"Sounds like he was a joker too, like this pair, 'how say you, Cousin Sally?' "

The elder Latimers found a hotel, the De Bussy, in the Rue Caumartin, and settled in very comfortably. They had two rooms, with a connecting door between, upon the third floor; they had no view from their windows since these looked out upon a light-well, but this did not trouble them since they did not mean to spend much time within doors. The porter withdrew and left the cousins alone.

"What shall we do first?" asked Charles.

"Unpack, of course. Then, by Jove I want a shave! So do you. There are small washing cabinets behind these curtains, most convenient. I wonder how one lights these lamps. At the Hôtel du Commerce, if you remember, one turned a small knob or protuberance through half a circle—these do not turn. Charles, how do these things work?"

Charles had wandered across to the window and was looking up at the roof three stories above. "There is a handsome balustrade surrounding this court; I have a great mind to go up there and walk along it."

"Charles, Charles! You will spoil it all. I cannot sufficiently emphasize the importance of our behaving in all respects like mortal men." James came to the connecting door and leaned a shoulder against the doorpost. "You will have us ejected for unseemly behavior."

Charles's eyes danced with laughter. "Dear James, does such a thing never happen to mortal men?"

"Not to me," said James. "That is—except—but that was all a misunderstanding—"

"I seem to remember a night when we were asked to leave Le Sphinx because you stood on a table to sing ' 'Twas in Trafalgar's Bay'!"

"That is all long ago," said James. "Besides, that was human enough. I was drunk. What I intended to convey, Cousin, was that anything which savors of the supernatural must be avoided at all costs."

"How dull!"

"Charles!"

"Oh, very well, Cousin. No tricks except in an emergency, eh?"

"Now come and examine the lighting arrangements," said James.

They shaved and changed; a card framed upon the wall near the door attracted Charles's attention.

"This room," he read aloud, "one thousand three hundred francs per night. You know, James, that hundred thousand francs will not support us in comfort for very long. We had best walk out and ascertain the whereabouts of a bank."

"We have enough for our present needs," said James mildly.

"Does your conscience reproach you, Cousin, at the thought of robbing a bank? We have done it once already."

"I know, Cousin, I know. I saw no alternative at that juncture, but I admit I find the memory galling."

"So do not I," said Charles energetically. "This is the country we died for, damn! They owe us something. Damn, sir, they did not even give us Christian burial!"

"Calm yourself, Charles, you are wasting energy. Yes, I dare say you are in the right, though to speak strictly by the letter, it is Prussia who owes us for our deaths, is it not? No matter. Perhaps we could go to Auteuil or Longchamps and back a winner."

"Or sit in at a game of cards. Let us find a nest of cardsharpers looking for a pigeon to pluck, then we need have no compunction in fleecing the wolves, eh, James?"

"Let us go out," said James, pulling down his waistcoat. "Did you notice how the porter worked that lift in which we ascended? He did not pull upon a rope."

"He pressed a button labeled 3 and the thing stopped of itself on this floor," said Charles. "Simple."

But when they reached the lift-shaft the lift was no longer there.

"I have it," said James. "The thing only works upwards and we are expected to walk down. It is easy, walking down."

"Surely," said Charles, "surely."

When they reached ground level, sure enough the lift was there; they glanced at it and nodded to each other. The porter saw it and came forward. Did the gentlemen not care to use the lift? It was only to press the button at the gate and the lift would come up, there was no need to summon him.

"Thank you, thank you," said James. "We walked down because we like walking."

"Exercise," said Charles, "is good for the figure." He smiled sweetly at the man and they walked out of the hotel.

"We shall have to be careful, Charles, or we shall make ourselves conspicuous.'

"Why not," said Charles innocently, "in Paris? Are Englishmen no longer considered mad?"

They strolled down the Rue Caumartin and came out upon the Boulevard des Capucines.

"I remember this well," said James happily. "The shops are very much improved, but I remember the street perfectly. To our right there is the Madeleine, to our left the Place de l'Opéra. Let us cross the boulevard, my dear Charles, as soon as there is opportunity; I have a fancy to walk once again in the gardens of the Tui—"

The Rue Caumartin is a one-way street entered from the Boulevard des Capucines. A taxi entering it at that moment did not, therefore, keep to its own side of the road; it cut the corner and whirled past within an inch of James's nose, startling him so much that he instantly vanished, to appear again, pale and shaken, in the doorway of a travel agency on the corner. Charles, overcome with laughter, joined him there in time to hear him being addressed by an elderly Englishwoman who was just coming out of the door.

"My good man!"

James swept off his hat and bowed deeply. "Ma'am, I hope so, indeed."

"Where—where did you come from?"

"Ma'am, from the road, where I have by a hair's breadth escaped destruction. If I had the misfortune to alarm you, ma'am"—another low bow—"I shall never forgive my deplorable lack of consideration."

"Mountebank!" said the lady, and swept past them.

James, with a puzzled line between his brows, slowly replaced his hat. "One would think, Charles, that I had insulted the lady. Nothing was further from my thoughts. I am sorry if I startled her; I could only apologize."

"You great booby," said Charles affectionately, "do you not know what you did? If you dematerialize like that and then pop up just in front of pious maiden ladies you will startle them."

"Oh, did I do that? I was not aware of it. How do you know she was pious?"

"She reminded me of your sister Emma, and heaven knows she is pious enough."

"True, true," said James with a reminiscent smile. "But a little piety is becoming to women. Well, shall we cross now?"

They reached the Tuileries Gardens without further mishap, decided to keep the Louvre for another day, and turned instead towards the Place de la Concorde. This historic spot delighted them, and no wonder, for the afternoon was fine, the fountains were playing and so was a band somewhere in the distance, all the passing motors hooted and a river steamer answered, and messenger boys whistled about their business. Paris was awaking from her summer siesta.

"We were right, Cousin," said James, "to seize upon the first opportunity to revisit this gay scene once more," but Charles was not attending to him.

"Here is the Métro of which Cousin Sally spoke. It is an underground railway like yours in London, except that there seems to be a great deal more of it. Look at the map, Cousin James. What curious names have some of these stations! Many of them would appear to be the names of famous men. Could Franklin D. Roosevelt possibly be an American, do you think?"

"No doubt the Metropolitan Railway in London is greatly extended by now," said James, but he looked interestedly at the map.

"Let us take a ride on this railway."

"Certainly, if you wish it, Charles."

Close against the head of the steps there was set up a stall where a woman was selling French National Lottery tickets. Even as they watched, several people came to her, bought tickets, and immediately went down the steps. James came to the obvious conclusion. "They are buying railway tickets," he said. "I will obtain some. Where shall we go?"

"Anywhere," said Charles cheerfully, "except Père Lachaise."

James laughed and addressed the ticket seller.

"Two tickets, if you please. How much is it to—"

"A hundred francs each, monsieur. Two hundred francs."

"But—are they all the same price?"

"Certainly, monsieur. All the same price."

He gave her the money, and as she plainly expected him to take up his own tickets he did so, tearing them off the counterfoils, and returned to Charles with them in his hand.

"This is an expensive mode of travel, Cousin. These colored scraps of paper cost me a hundred francs each."

"Indeed? It must be very luxurious."

They went down the stairs together and were stopped at the barrier by the ticket collector, a stout elderly woman with a face like a wizened apple. James offered her the tickets.

"But, monsieur! These are not travel tickets. These are lottery tickets, *voyez-vous!*" She laughed kindly and pointed out the inscription upon the tickets, *Loterie Nationale Française.*

"Oh, excuse me," said James, covered with confusion. "How excessively stupid—I did not observe— " He crumpled the lottery tickets in his hand. "Where do I buy the proper ones?"

"Oh, monsieur! Do not throw them away! The draw is tonight and you may win a prize."

"Indeed. I think the chance is very remote," said James, but he flattened out the tickets and put them carefully into his pocketbook. "How shall I—where are the results posted?"

"They will be in all the Paris papers, or any bartender will tell Monsieur which are the lucky numbers. Over there, look, the ticket office and the tickets are thirty francs wherever you wish to go.

"Only the one price?"

"Only the one price. It is easy to see that the gentlemen are strangers to Paris."

"Well, not quite," said the truthful James, "but it is indeed very many years since we were here."

"Since you were very little boys, eh? Naturally, you do not remember about such things as railway tickets. Look, for this ticket which you shall buy you can travel all day round Paris if you wish, only if you come up to the surface do you give it up. Understood?"

"You know, Cousin," said Charles as they walked away down the passage leading to the platforms, "that good old soul probably thinks she is old enough to be our mother. Whereas— Is this where we await the trains? It looks like a platform. There is a noise coming— James!"

They recoiled together as, with a rising roar, the train rushed into the station and clattered to a stop. Doors clashed open; people leapt out and made for the exit, taking no notice whatever of the Latimers. Before they could decide what they ought to do the grinding doors slid together again and the train ran noisily away out of sight.

CHAPTER VII:

Ulysses

THE LATIMERS gained courage when other intending passengers came on their platform at the Concorde Métro station and after one or two false starts managed to enter a train. There followed an interval of delicious terror comparable only with a small boy's first ride on a switchback.

"There is one thing I would dearly like to know," said James when the excitement had begun to abate, "and that is how anyone knows at which station they have arrived."

"I wonder that myself," said Charles. "It is a strange thing, Cousin, that they should all be named Dubonnet. Even before one actually reaches the station there it is, illuminated on the wall, Dubonnet. Of the cap? What is this 'of the cap' everywhere?"

James noticed an advertisement which gave rather more details, and pointed it out. "It is a medicine, that is all," he said. "An advertisement of a medicine. If we look more carefully we shall find the names of the stations also."

Charles lost interest in Dubonnet. "Let us change at the next stop," he said. "I think that a station marked *'Correspondance' is* one where several lines meet."

It was only a short step from this to becoming thoroughly lost, and after a time the noise and the atmosphere began to make themselves felt.

"Let us return to the upper air upon the next occasion of stopping," said James. "This continual roar of sound is becoming irksome, how say you, Charles?"

"I am with you, James. There is also a peculiar smell," said Charles thoughtfully. "Let us return, as you say, to the upper air once again."

At the next stop they leapt out; the station was Sablons, which meant nothing to them until they emerged into the sunshine.

"I know where we are," said James, his eyes resting gratefully upon green grass and ordered plantations of tall trees. "This is the Bois de Boulogne; we used to ride here in the mornings to take the air and scrutinize the ladies. Let us go in; it is quiet and pleasant here."

"I recall it well, Cousin. There was one dazzling brunette who took your eye, I remember, she used to ride a bay——"

"I was in mourning for my poor wife," said James hastily. "There are some greenhouses here, shall we turn towards them? I greatly admire greenhouses and I do not recall ever having visited these."

"As you wish," said Charles absently. "She wore a brown velvet habit, did she not, and in her hat a brown feather which came down to her shoulder."

"I should be interested indeed to see if they have any new cacti. My collection of cacti——"

"I cannot charge my memory with her name," said Charles, snapping his fingers impatiently.

"I was mourning my wife," said James firmly.

Beyond the hothouses there are the monkeys. Everyone has seen

monkeys in cages; restless, inconsequent, preternaturally wise, and cata-
strophically silly. James, who had had two sons of his own, strolled along
watching the children who rushed madly about, occasionally stopping
abruptly to look into the cages. Charles pushed his broad-brimmed hat
to the back of his head and drifted along, the picture of lazy amusement.

A small boy emerged from a side alley, came towards the cousins
until he was quite close, and then looked up at them and stopped suddenly to stare.

"Eh bien, mon petit," said Charles, who was the subject of this attention. "What is it, then?"

The child pointed with a stubby finger. "Did you get him out of one
of the cages?"

"Good lack!" said James, following the direction of the finger. "God
bless my soul!"

Charles put his hand up to his own shoulder and encountered a
small hairy paw.

"Gentlemen, hush! Oh, my stars!"

"How did that happen?"

"It seems that Ulysses also has met with some relations," said Charles.
"I ought to have thought of that before we came here."

"I did not know there were any monkeys here," said James in a pained
voice, "until I saw them."

"I saw something about zoology upon a notice board," admitted
Charles, "but I never thought of this. No, sir, the idea never occurred to
me that with monkeys, as with us, the presence of a member of the same
family would permit materialization." They walked on together with the
small boy running beside them to stare open-mouthed at Ulysses in his
little red jacket and round cap. Presently the monkey noticed the small
boy's interest, took off his little cap, and bowed profoundly. The child
fled.

"This principle of family," argued James, "surely cannot be applied
in the case of monkeys, who have no sense of family and are, indeed,
entirely promiscuous?"

"Maybe that is why just any monkeys would do. Why are we distress-
ing ourselves? I always liked to have Ulysses around and I still do, so
what?"

"If anything alarms him, what will he do?"

"The same as you do, Cousin, I reckon. Vanish."

"I can foresee a whole series of embarrassing situations," said James
gloomily.

There came the sound of a shrill voice in one of the adjacent alleys explaining to someone called Maman that the speaker was not telling stories, indeed no. There was a man with a monkey sitting on his shoulder; he got it out of one of the cages. Maman saw an attendant at a little distance and rushed to meet him.

"Let us deal with them if and when they arise," said Charles. "Come down off my shoulder, Ulysses. Why should I carry you on such a hot day? Take my hand and walk properly. Consider, Cousin James. Suppose a man thinks he sees a monkey in some place where no monkey should be, in a box at the Opéra, for example. Then suppose the monkey to vanish in an instant of time, completely. Is that man going to proclaim what he thought he saw? Would you, Cousin James?"

"No, hang me if I would!"

"Well, there you are."

"Monsieur!" cried Maman. "Monsieur le Gardien! There is one of your monkeys loose."

"What?" said the attendant. "Are you sure? Where?"

"Over there," said the child. "With those two men there."

He pointed as Charles and James came into view with Ulysses walking demurely beside them.

"I will myself regulate this matter," said the attendant. He dashed into a small shed nearby and came out again with a contrivance like a butterfly net, only larger and with a coarse string-mesh bag.

"Are you going to catch it? Are you going to catch it with that? Maman, he is going to catch—"

The attendant advanced with purposeful strides.

"Achille, my son!" shrieked Maman. "Come away, do not approach, the animal is savage! My only joy—"

"Let go, Maman! Let me go—I want to see the man catch the monkey—"

"Achille, thou art naughty—"

"I shall bite!"

"Messieurs," said the attendant, addressing the Latimers, "it is strictly forbidden to bring animals into the Zoological Gardens."

Ulysses removed his hat, placed the other tiny paw over his heart, and bowed deeply. Charles Latimer turned a kindly but puzzled look upon the attendant.

"Why, certainly," said the Virginian. "I should say, sir, that that is a very wise rule, yes, sir. Very right."

"Perfectly justifiable," said James loftily, and made to move on.

"But," said the attendant, and pointed at Ulysses.

"He is pointing at something, Cousin," said James.

"So I notice, Cousin," answered Charles. "What can it be?"

"It is a monkey," howled the attendant. "A Capuchin monkey with a red jacket and cap."

A series of bloodcurdling yells rent the air as Maman picked up Achille bodily and bore him, kicking and biting, out of sight.

"A monkey?" said Charles. "In a red jacket? Are you sure the jacket is red?"

"Poor man, poor man," said James in a low but perfectly audible tone.

"Tell me," said Charles with his charming smile, "is it your duty to attend to monkeys continuously, every day? All day?"

"Of course it is," replied the attendant. "Do you suppose do not know a *Cebus capucinus* when I see it?"

The Latimers looked at each other. "It is the sun," said James.

"Come, friend," said Charles pityingly. "Come and sit in the shade. Tell me where I can find a glass of water for you."

"All your monkeys are safely in their cages," added James reassuringly.

Ulysses, tired of standing still, jumped up and down, and the attendant lost his temper. He produced, with a swish, the monkey net from behind his back and whirled it over Ulysses, pinning him to the ground. There was a terrified "Eek!" a momentary vision of writhing arms and legs, and the net dropped flat and empty upon the sandy path.

The attendant shook his head, turned upon his heel, and walked slowly and dispiritedly away.

* * * *

Upon the following day James and Charles Latimer went to the Ambassador Hotel to call upon Jeremy and Sally, but they were out. "They are lunching with friends," said the porter. "They told me that they would return during the afternoon. If the gentlemen would care to wait—"

He indicated, with a wave of his hand, the spacious lounge of the Ambassador Hotel across the end of the entrance hall; the cousins nodded and strolled on together.

"There is a bar, James," said Charles Latimer, looking away to his right. "Shall we take a glass of wine while we wait?"

James nodded. "You might obtain your mint julep here, Charles. It looks to me the sort of place where they would have everything."

They went up the two steps and entered the bar, almost empty at the hour of early afternoon. Away to the right two men were sitting at a table together talking in low tones; near the door an elderly man was sitting upon a stool with his elbows on the bar, talking to the bartender in English. The Latimers sat down nearby and Charles asked for a mint julep; the bartender nodded and began to prepare it.

The elderly man turned stiffly upon his stool and surveyed them. White hair surmounted a face which looked as though it had been dyed with permanganate of potash and afterwards varnished; a stiff yellowish mustache ended in waxed points. He looked from one Latimer to the other and eventually addressed Charles in an odd jerky voice, as though there were a comma between each of his words.

"You, sir, are an American, if I mistake not."

"Why, yes, sir, that is so. I am an American."

"Then it is no use my asking your advice about wines. I believe you drink only cocktails in your country. You, sir," to James, "are you an American too?"

"No, sir. No, I am an Englishman."

"Then perhaps you will be able to settle an argument between George and myself," indicating the bartender.

"George says that it is wrong to drink port after brandy. I say it is right. Every gentleman drinks port after lunch. I have had lunch and I propose to drink port. Eh? Am I not right?"

George came back with Charles Latimer's drink in a tall glass with the fresh mint leaves clinging to the rim. "The Colonel," he said in a low tone, "has had quite enough already and it would be much better if he did not have any more."

"What are you saying?" asked the Colonel. "What are you saying? Are you talking about me?"

"George was saying that you are a distinguished Army officer," said James. "May I ask, sir, if you have seen much service?"

The old Colonel pushed up his mustache. "A few minor brawls, sir, in the service of the British Raj. Nothing spectacular, nothing spectacular. Chasing dacoits through the jungle, sir. George, port!"

"In a moment, sir," said George, busy with glasses.

"That must have been quite exciting," said James.

"Exciting! Huh! I suppose you might call it exciting never to know, from one minute to the next, when you'd get your backside peppered with hobnails from a yard of gas pipe tied to a tree."

James looked so completely blank that even the Colonel noticed it.

"You are not an Army man, I take it? No? Well, we can't all do what we should like. But I asked your opinion about port. Can one drink it after brandy or can one not? I say one can, provided it is after lunch. Or dinner, of course."

"With respect, sir," said James, "I should say not. Either brandy or port, but not, I should think, both."

The Colonel merely looked at him contemptuously and crooked

his finger for George, who came as slowly as was feasible.

"A glass of the same port I had last night."

"Very good, sir."

"And hurry up with it! Damn, sir," to James, "the way young men dawdle about in these days makes me sick! Wish I had some of 'em in my troop in the old days, I'd make 'em jump to it!"

George brought the glass of port and put it down in front of the Colonel, who set it aside for a moment while he fumbled for his wallet to pay for the wine.

"When I was in India as a very young man, sir, we were taught how to maintain discipline. Of course things were very different then."

"I do not doubt it, sir."

George asked James Latimer what he would take; James said he would have a glass of red wine, please.

"Côte-du-Rhône?" said George. "a 1937?"

James nodded trustfully and turned back to the Colonel, who was sorting out grimy currency notes and talking all the time.

"No motor transport in those days, of course. If there had been it wouldn't have stood up to the roads. Damn these filthy notes; I say the French make them sticky on purpose in the hope you'll pay them two at once. No electric light, only stinking oil lamps. No telephones, of course. Sir, I remember when the electric light was first installed at one place where I was stationed. They strung up insulated cables on poles; I could have told 'em what would happen. It did. All the monkeys came out of the jungle and swung along the wires, dozens of 'em, sir, dozens of 'em." His gnarled, uncertain fingers stiffened and he stared incredulously at his glass. "I said monkeys, sir, I said monkeys. God bless my soul, sir, there's one of the little b-beasts on the bar now."

George, who had turned away to pour James's wine, spun round sharply just in time to see a small Capuchin monkey, dressed in a little red jacket and a tiny round cap, taking a careful sip from the Colonel's glass. He set it down, rose, and bowed politely to the Colonel, raising his cap. Then he seized the glass in both hands and lifted it to his mouth. As he did so he seemed to the horrified George to shimmer and thin out like smoke until there was nothing left but a wineglass hanging in the air and tilting till all the wine in it had disappeared. Then there was a crash as the empty glass fell upon the bar counter and broke into a dozen pieces. The Colonel's eyes bulged. He got down, very stiff and dignified, from his stool and the currency notes fell disregarded from his hands.

"A monkey in a red jacket. A monkey——"

He turned as smartly as though he were on parade and marched out of the bar, down the steps, and across the lounge towards the lifts, not looking to right or left. There came the sound of clashing gates and the whine of an ascending lift; the Colonel had retired to his own room.

By this time George was at the bar counter, leaning heavily upon it.

"Excuse me, please. Did either of you two gentlemen see anything?"

James merely looked blank and Charles said: "What sort of thing do you mean?"

"The Colonel, sir, said that he saw a monkey sitting on the bar. Did either of you gentlemen see it?"

They shook their heads and Charles said that they were temperate men. "I gather, from a remark you passed earlier, that the Colonel was due to start seeing things 'most any time now.

"But I saw it too," said George, and wiped the perspiration from his forehead.

"Come, come, my man," said James. "Come, come."

"I did, sir. It picked up the glass, drank the wine, and let the glass fall on the counter. There are the broken pieces to prove it."

"Then where has it gone?" asked Charles, looking about him and down upon the floor.

"It did not go anywhere, sir. It"—George gestured with his hands—"it, as it were, thinned out and vanished."

Charles merely gaped at him and James said, "Most irregular, most," in a melancholy voice.

George snatched up his dustpan and brush and swept the broken glass off the counter. On second thoughts he rescued from the debris the base of the glass, which had survived with an inch of stem, and set it upon a shelf at the back of the bar. He gathered up the Colonel's money, still lying on the counter where he had left it, and began to stack the notes into a neat bundle.

The glass doors of the bar swung open and a cheerful voice behind them said, "Well, well, Sally, look who's here. Cousin James and Cousin Charles, I'm delighted that you should have come around to look us up. What are you having? George, this one is on me."

"Cousin Jeremy—ma'am—we took the chance of finding you at home. I hope you have recovered, ma'am, from the fatigue of the journey."

"I have indeed, thank you. Completely. And I have to thank one or both of you, haven't I, for the perfectly lovely flowers which came up to my room this morning? It was sweet of you and I adore carnations."

"Sweets to the sweet," said James with a bow.

"Ma'am, we saw them and immediately thought of you," said Charles. "It was inevitable. Pray sit here."

"What will Madame take?" asked George.

"Orange juice, please, George— Why, whatever is the matter? Darling, George does look queer."

"Thank you, madame. I do feel a little queer. I have just seen a monkey."

Sally drew back and clapped her hand over her mouth.

"Why," said Jeremy, "do you take an exception to monkeys, George? Don't you like 'em? Nice little beasts; a friend of mine back home has one as a pet. Why, did someone bring one into the bar?"

"No one brought it," said George in a tragic voice, "no one took it away. It came—"

"Are you telling me," said Jeremy, looking about him, "that it's running loose about here someplace? Look, why doesn't somebody do something about it, then? Try to catch it, or something?"

"Look," said George. He whirled round, picked the broken stem off the shelf, and smacked it down upon the counter. "You see this remains of a broken glass? Well—"

He unfolded his tale.

"But, George, what you are telling us is just impossible," said Jeremy.

"I know, sir, but—"

"George," said Sally, "may I change my mind? I won't have orange juice after all, I'd rather have a cognac."

"Certainly, madame." He picked up a liqueur glass and went to get the brandy.

"You feeling all right, honey? You look a bit white."

"I'm all right, thank you. Please don't fuss, I expect it's the heat. Oh, Cousin Charles, thank you."

Charles had brought a chair. "You will find this more restful than that high stool. Pray take my arm; there, that is better. Do not let this odd little story distress you, ma'am," he went on in a lower tone. "Believe me, there is some quite rational explanation."

She smiled and nodded and Jeremy came with the cognac.

"Will you just drink this, Sally dear, and take it easy for a bit. Then we'll go up to our rooms and you can lie down for an hour. It's the heat," he explained to James. "We've spent a couple of hours, in the middle of a day like this, going round some racing stables at Auteuil belonging to some friends of ours. It was quite a trail, and every stall and loosebox we came to we had to be introduced to each quadruped personally. Cousin James, sir, it put me in mind of my old grandfather— my mother's father—reading family prayers in the old house near Charlottesville. Abinadab begat Jehoiakim and Jehoiakim begat somebody else, and so it went on. So did these horses. Yes, sir. Feeling better, honey?"

CHAPTER VIII:
The Lottery Ticket

JEREMY LATIMER went away with an arm round Sally, and the company looked after them.

"A very nice lady," said George. He realized that his monkey story was not going down well with anybody and made a determined effort to behave normally.

"I hope," said Charles Latimer rather anxiously, "that all is well with our charming cousin."

"Young wives," said James sententiously, "are apt to become subject to these trifling distempers."

George picked up the Colonel's pile of notes and began to sort them in order of value. A gaily colored counterfoil fluttered out from among them. "The Colonel," said the bartender, "has bought a lottery ticket." He put the money into an envelope, scribbled the Colonel's name upon it, and locked it away in a drawer. "I wonder whether he has won anything." He ran his finger down a closely printed paragraph in a newspaper. "No. The poor gentleman has had no luck."

"We have some of those tickets, Cousin," said Charles, "if you have not mislaid them."

"I laid them in my pocketbook. Here they are. Are these any good?"

James pushed them across the counter and George looked them up. "That one also is no good. Now the other. Just a moment! The number, again? Ah!" A cry of triumph which drew the attention of the two men at the far end. "This is marvelous! The first prize! Monsieur is wonderfully lucky! Congratulations, monsieur!"

"The f-first prize?" stammered James. "Indeed! How very unexpected. And how providential, eh, Charles? How much is it?"

"One million francs, monsieur! Look for yourself."

"I am all abroad," said James. "One milli—Did you say one million?"

"Francs, Cousin, francs," said Charles. "I opine it sounds more than it really it, but," with an excited laugh, "even so I guess it is quite a sizable sum, yes, sir. Tell me, George, what is that in English pounds? I am so excited that I cannot calculate."

"A little over a thousand pounds sterling, sir."

James made a mental note that French francs were just under one thousand to the pound.

"That will help out with your currency allowance, sir?"

"What? Oh yes, yes, no doubt," said James vaguely. "Let us have a round of drinks on this. Cousin Charles, what is your fancy? Tapster, you will drink with me? These gentlemen over there—Sirs, I have had a stroke of luck, I beg that you will celebrate it with me. Pray order whatever you may desire. This is a great day."

The two men rose, smiling, from their table and came up to the bar. They were not, when seen at close hand, particularly prepossessing; although they appeared to be only in their thirties, their faces were lined and their mouths hard and thin-lipped. However, they were well dressed and their manners were easy and friendly.

"Congratulations," said one, and shook James warmly by the hand. "Good luck, sir, jolly good luck."

"I do congratulate you, sir," said the other, and also shook hands. "One sees the names of prizewinners in the press, but this is the very first time I have met one in the flesh. It's encouraging to be assured that prizewinners really do exist and are not just another name for some of the organizers or their friends."

"Gentlemen," said George reproachfully, "these lotteries are run by the French Government and their bona-fides are beyond question."

"That's what I was afraid of," said the second man. "Things which no one ever questions are apt to be a bit—you know."

"Do you mean," said James anxiously, "that you think I may not receive my winnings?"

"Ah no, sir, I am sure that that will be all right. Now you hold the winning ticket you are safe, provided you don't lose the ticket."

James put it away carefully in his pocketbook while his new friends ordered cherry brandies. Charles looked the two men over and what he saw appeared to amuse him, for the corners of his mouth curled up.

"You gentlemen are residents in this hotel?" he asked.

"No. No, we are staying for a few days in a small hotel near the Madeleine. We came in here this afternoon to meet a friend, but he doesn't seem to be coming."

"Provoking," said Charles. "To wait for someone who does not come, it is a waste of time."

The other shrugged his shoulders. "It is all a waste of time, our stay in Paris. We ought to be in Germany but for our own silly fault." He laughed. "Really, for men who travel quite a lot, we ought to be kicked. We allowed our German visas to expire—never looked at the damn things—and got turned back on the frontier. Never felt such a fool in my life."

"By Jove," said James, "most disconcerting, upon my word. Do you mean to tell me that the rogues actually refused to let you pass?"

The man laughed aloud. "That's good, that is. 'The rogues refused to let us pass.' De Garth, did you hear that?"

"I did," said De Garth, much amused.

"But what course of action did you pursue?" asked James.

"Well, what would you have done?"

"Summoned the British Consul, of course," said James sturdily.

"Sir," said De Garth, "I wish you were traveling with us. No journey could be dull in your company. May we introduce ourselves? My name's De Garth, as you may have noticed, and my friend's is Fosse."

James bowed. "Our name is Latimer. I am James Latimer and this is my cousin Major Latimer."

"Of the British Army?"

"No, sir," said Charles. "I have the honor to be an American. I come from Virginia."

"And is this your first visit to Paris, Major Latimer?"

"By no means, but it is many years since I and my cousin were here.

"We—er—had an opportunity of spending a short vacation here," said James, "and we were happy to avail ourselves of it. Excuse me, I see your glasses are empty. George!" Fosse protested, but James bore him down. "It is not every day that one has such a stroke of luck."

"I must say," said Fosse, "that you have made good use of your time, winning a prize like that. What do you do with yourselves all day long?"

James said that they had only arrived the previous day and so far they had simply walked about enjoying the sights. "We propose a visit to the Musée du Louvre to improve our minds with a study of some of the greatest artistic triumphs of antiquity, and we hope to pay a visit to the Opéra upon the occasion of the performance of some classical work."

"Mr. Latimer," said De Garth with something like reverence, "how do you do it?"

James stared and Charles came to the rescue.

"Sir, I will not deny that we propose also to amuse ourselves with a little frivolity. Tell me, sir, is there not a place of entertainment called the Bal Tabarin?"

"You'll do," said the enraptured Fosse, "you'll do. There's also a quiet little show called the Folies Bergère you might cast your eyes over sometime."

"Sir, I am obliged to you," said Charles. "How do men of your type in Paris usually pass your time?"

"Well," said De Garth, "we're here on business as a rule, though we're rather at a loose end this time. We generally like to get one or two pals together and have a game of cards in the evening. Do either of you gentlemen care for a hand of cards?"

Charles shook his head and said that he was never a cardplayer, but James said that he had been considered a fair performer at basset in his time. "But that is considered old-fashioned now, I know, and whist is all the rage. I have had many a pleasant evening playing whist."

"We generally play a simple and even childish game called poker," said Fosse.

"If it is really as simple as you say perhaps I could manage to learn it," said James.

"If we could get a few of the boys together," said Fosse, addressing De Garth, "we might manage to give Mr. Latimer an hour or two of quiet amusement."

"Or there's rummy, if we can't get hold of anyone," said De Garth. "That is also quite simple to a man of Mr. Latimer's attainments."

"Let's make a date," said Fosse. "Tomorrow night at our hotel? We've got a little sitting-room where we can be private."

James accepted. "I take it very kindly of you, gentlemen, to admit a total stranger to your private gathering. I shall be delighted to come and I trust you will not find me too stupid to learn a new game."

"And your cousin, Major Latimer—"

"Gentlemen, I thank you," said Charles, "but no, if you will excuse me. I have already an engagement for tomorrow night. Besides, if I may admit what practically amounts to a social solecism, cards bore me. My cousin here is your man."

They exchanged addresses before De Garth and Fosse took their leave, saying they would wait no longer for their expected friend. "Either there's been a mistake or he's been run over by a taxi," said Fosse cheerfully. "We are all mortal, especially in Paris."

They went away, not speaking together until they were well away from the Ambassador's splendid portals, when De Garth turned to Fosse.

"What the devil are they? Just plain goofy?"

Fosse nodded. "If you ask me, they've escaped from somewhere, but why worry? The stodgy one has got a million francs, hasn't he?"

"He looks harmless enough; I'm not so sure about the other."

"Well, he's not coming, so that's all right. We'll have Roux in; he'll deal with him if he makes trouble. A million francs!"

"He's a birthday present, if only he knew it," said De Garth.

James paid for the rounds of drinks when Charles refused another.

"Gentlemen," said George, "if it is not taking a liberty—"

"What is it?"

"It might be as well to be a little careful in playing cards with those two. Not that I have heard any complaints about them, but they make a practice of sitting in this bar and picking acquaintance with any who appear to have money. I do not wish to interfere with the gentlemen's amusements."

James smiled and Charles laughed aloud. "That is kind of you, George," he said, "and we surely do appreciate it. But we are not, maybe, so young as we look. We will take precautions."

"I thought you said you were not going, sir?"

"I said so, George, I certainly said so. Yes, sir. But we shall see when the time comes. Cousin James, the afternoon is pleasant, let us take the air."

"Certainly," said James. "Whatever you say, Cousin. Good day to you, George. No doubt we shall meet again."

"I hope so, sir," said George. He leaned on the bar and watched them cross the lounge on the way out, two tall men wearing their hats with an air which appealed to him.

"Those two," he murmured, "are assuredly something a little different. *Ce sont des railleurs.* I like them. But that monkey—"

On the following evening James and Charles left the De Bussy Hotel together, but when James reached the hotel where De Garth and Fosse awaited him, he was alone. Fosse was waiting in the hall to greet him.

"Splendid, so glad to see you. Do come up. This is rather a dingy place, but conveniently central. Let's take the lift. We have a grubby little sitting-room upstairs, but at least we can be private."

"I am sure, Mr. Fosse, that it will all be quite delightful. One cannot expect, when traveling, the elegant refinements of home, but a decent privacy is in itself a matter for congratulation."

Fosse opened his mouth and shut it again and the lift stopped. He led the way along a dark and narrow corridor and flung open a door at the end.

"Here we are, De Garth, all present an' correct. Mr. Latimer, may I introduce a friend of ours, Monsieur le Comte d'Autun, who also enjoys a pleasant game of cards. D'Autun, Mr. James Latimer."

The man called D'Autun said that he was enchanted, James said that he was honored, and both bowed. D'Autun was a small man with black hair going thin on the top, spiky black eyebrows and mustache, and black hair on the backs of his hands. He was not very like James's idea of a French count with a territorial title, but no doubt even French counts come all shapes. James smiled to himself and waited politely for Monsieur le Comte to sit down before he seated himself. Wine was poured out for the company and there was a little discussion as to what they should play. They were not enough to play poker; one needs six players at least and more if possible. James smiled, agreed with everything that was said, and amused himself by shuffling the pack which lay before him. He shuffled with great dexterity, the cards appearing to flow from one hand to the other.

"What d'you suggest, Mr. Latimer?"

"You are my hosts," said James. "I would prefer that you should decide. Indeed, I have no preference except, perhaps, for a keen game of *écarté.*"

It was quite plain that none of the party had ever heard of *écarté* and they proceeded, by means of a few exhibition hands, to teach him to play rummy.

"Thank you," said James at length, "I think I have now grasped the rudiments of this very interesting pastime. If I should make mistakes, pray do me the favor of pointing them out.

The evening proceeded as such evenings do. James, who had a flair for card-playing, did not make mistakes; the first few games were reasonably even and then he began to win. He won consistently until there was quite a pile of thousand franc notes at his elbow.

"Really, gentlemen," said James, "your luck tonight has gone out to chase moonbeams. Monsieur le Comte, you will take me for a Jeremy Diddler, a bubbler, upon my honor."

Monsieur le Comte merely stared, but Fosse broke into a loud laugh. "Fortune favors the bold," he said. "Let's double the stakes, shall we? De Garth, O.K.? D'Autun, you agree? That is, if our guest agrees?"

"Certainly, certainly," said James. "I think it is your deal, De Garth."

"And D'Autun shuffles," agreed Fosse. "Let me refill the glasses."

He rose to do so and in so doing turned his back towards a small table upon which James's hat was lying and which was for the moment within James's view alone. The hat rose suddenly a couple of inches from the table and at once alighted again. James smiled amiably and settled down lower in his chair as Fosse handed him his refilled glass and De Garth began to deal.

"You know," said James, "it was prodigiously civil of you to ask me here tonight. I cannot think when I have enjoyed an evening more. Such good—"

"The evening's not over yet, Latimer, the night is yet young, to quote the poet."

"I am glad of it; there is time for me to give you your revenge. Such good wine, too, quite delectable. I must ask you for the address of your wine merchant, my dear Fosse. I am not much of a tippler as a rule—"

"But rules are made to be broken sometimes, aren't they?" said Fosse with his horse laugh.

"I am of your opinion. Crack a bottle and break a rule, eh?" James picked up the hand which had been dealt him. "Now let us see what the random jade, my Lady Luck, has for me this time."

Whether Luck was annoyed at being called rude names or whether there was another reason for it, James began to lose from that moment and lost steadily. The pile of notes at his elbow lessened and vanished and he had recourse to a bulging wallet which made Monsieur le Comte open his eyes very wide.

"It is as well," said James with his sudden barking laugh, "that I cashed that lottery ticket this morning. Otherwise, gentlemen, I should have had to cry you mercy." He glanced at his watch. "As it is, and if you are agreeable, shall we double the stakes again?"

"Que diable!" said the Count, speaking for almost the first time. "You are a hell of a good loser."

"You relieve my anxiety, sir," said James. "It is true that I am losing my money, but I thought you must have gambled away your tongue."

The Count's stiff eyebrows drew together, but De Garth intervened. "Monsieur D'Autun was always one of the quiet ones."

"No babbler," said James. "Sir, I applaud him for it. If one has nothing to say, why say it?"

The Count's thick neck reddened, but Fosse passed him the shuffled pack. "Your deal, D'Autun."

"I thought perhaps doubling the stakes might have done for me what it did for you," said James half an hour later, "but it seems not. Out of common humanity towards the landlord of my hotel, I must cry a halt soon."

"Of course," said Fosse instantly, "whenever you wish." Since they had won nearly seven hundred pounds of James's money even those three sharks did not wish to press him too far. "If our German visas don't come through in a day or two, perhaps you'll come and have your revenge."

"If I win another lottery prize," laughed James.

De Garth collected together the money on the table, put it in a small attache case, and snapped the lock shut. He opened a door on the farther side of the room and went into what was evidently a bedroom.

James was very plainly noticing nothing.

"I have in mind a visit to Auteuil tomorrow in an endeavour to recoup my losses," he was saying cheerfully. "My cousin, whom you met, is knowledgeable about horseflesh; I shall lean upon his guidance."

"I wish you all the luck in the world," said Fosse warmly. "You thoroughly deserve it."

There came the sound of a closing drawer and De Garth returned, leaving the bedroom door ajar.

"Not at all," said James, "not at all. 'Today to thee, tomorrow to me,' as the Spanish say. Well, gentlemen, all good things come to an end at last." They heard a muffled thump from the next room, but James took no notice. "It only remains for me to express how greatly obliged I am to you for a —"

"One moment," said Fosse, and went with long strides into the next room. They could all hear him pulling open one drawer and then another.

"De Garth!" he called. "Which drawer did you put that money in?"

"Left-hand top, as usual," answered De Garth, and followed Fosse into the bedroom.

"Charming people," said James, addressing the Count. "Such ease of manner, such an aura of integrity and honor. Without doubt they are men of the best families." He picked up his hat.

"Without doubt," said the Count, edging away.

"I should like to add what a privilege I feel it, to have been enabled to meet, informally like this, a representative of one of the great French territorial families in your distinguished person."

There could be heard from the next room the sound of an argument in progress; the actual words were inaudible, but the tone of the voices sounded angry. Cupboard doors opened and shut. The Count was so interested in this that he failed to answer James's mellifluous politeness.

"These gentlemen," pursued James, "are, no doubt, old friends of yours. Boyhood friends, perhaps? Or even relatives? It is easy to see that you are all, as we say, horses of the same color."

The baited Count looked despairingly towards the bedroom door, but instead of rescue there came from it only Fosse's voice raised in fury.

"Here it is and it's empty! For the last time, Slick, *where have you put it?*"

" 'Slick,' " repeated James. "Delightful, to hear the sobriquets of childhood persisting throughout the—"

"I haven't got it, I tell you," said De Garth desperately. "I put it in that case and put the case in that drawer. You moved it yourself when you came in."

"Then it's that twister Roux," said Fosse. He and De Garth came out with a rush, seized upon the alleged Count, and hastily searched him for a packet of notes which would certainly not be easily concealed. Roux protested angrily and James intervened.

"Gentlemen, gentlemen!" He flapped his hat at them as though they were intrusive hens. "What has occasioned this regrettable—"

"All that money! It's gone!"

"I haven't touched it," whined Roux. "I never went near the bed-room, I didn't."

"It is, indeed, quite impossible that Monsieur le Comte could be concerned in this peculiar affair," said James.

This was so plainly true that De Garth and Fosse let him go and turned to face each other.

"Then it must be you," they said simultaneously, in exact duet, and immediately war broke out. They aimed wild blows at each other which, one would have said, had both missed their mark since the men had obviously no idea how to use their fists. Yet there were a couple of crisp thuds and they staggered apart, De Garth with a hand up to a damaged eye and Fosse holding his jaw. They rushed together again, Fosse slapped De Garth hard across the face, and De Garth kicked him savagely on the shin.

"Come, Monsieur le Comte," said James, taking Roux by the elbow. "This scene is repugnant to men of refinement, let us go."

He whirled Roux towards the door. It proved to be locked, but the key was in it. James opened it and took the key out, pulled Roux out of the room, and locked the door after them. Just outside the door there was a flight of service stairs.

James took the key out of the lock and tossed it down the stairwell.

CHAPTER IX:

A Matter of Passports

"I THINK WE WILL not wait for the lift," said James. He put his arm through Roux's and ran him down the stairs.

"But," said Roux, jibbing, "where are we going? I want to go back. I—I have forgotten something."

"We are going to a café for a little glass of something to take the taste of that out of our mouths. Or a cup of coffee, if you prefer it. I cannot believe that you really wish to return to that sharpers' den."

At this moment Roux became aware that there was a third set of footsteps just behind him on the stairs. He turned and looked straight into the laughing face of another tall man close upon his heels.

"Besides, we want to talk to you," said the newcomer.

"Who are you?" gasped Roux. "Police?"

"No, no," said James. "Dear me, no. This gentleman is my cousin.

We had an idea that there might be a little trouble there this evening, so he came to call for me and escort me home. That is all."

They emerged upon the street, very close together, with Roux in the middle. He noticed that Charles Latimer had a cardboard shoebox under his arm.

"There is a café almost opposite," said Charles, "upon that corner. It looks reasonably clean, how say you, Cousin?"

"I dare say that it will serve," said James indifferently.

They entered it and found a table in a corner where they could speak without being overheard, and gave their order. Before the waiter came back with the drinks Charles opened the shoebox and took a handful of notes from an incredibly fat roll with a rubber band round it. Roux looked at it and his eyes bulged, then he rose precipitately from his seat and made to go.

"Sit down," said James sharply. 'What ails you, man?"

Roux nodded towards the roll of notes. "It is magic," he said. "It is sorcery. That is the roll of notes which disappeared from the bedroom back there."

Charles laughed. "Nonsense, sir, nonsense. One roll of notes is just like another. What's bitten you?"

"The band. The rubber band, it's theirs. They always use it for their winnings."

The notes were held together by a broad rubber band of mingled colors of red and white.

"You are moonstruck," said Charles contemptuously. "What, will you tell me that bands such as this are made only for Messieurs Fosse and de Garth? Sir, I bought half a dozen like this in Brentano's this morning."

"Oh," said Roux in a flat voice. "Indeed. Yes, I suppose you could." He sat down again and sipped his *fine*; he seemed to find it comforting.

"These little coincidences," said Charles easily, "I allow, can be disconcerting. Yes, sir. Waiter! A length of string if you please. I want to tie up this cardboard box."

"Now tell me," said James, leaning back in his chair and turning a daunting stare upon Roux, "you were brought into that party tonight to help to fleece me, were you not?"

Roux nodded.

"And your name is Roux, is it?"

"Gaston Roux."

"And you are no more the Comte d'Autun than I am the Pope of Rome?"

"That is so, monsieur."

"But why D'Autun?" asked Charles, idly twirling his glass by the stem.

"I come from Autun, monsieur, it was my birthplace. So, when Autun is mentioned it is easy to remember that it is I who am being addressed."

"I see. A variety of aliases would tend to confuse you?"

"Yes, monsieur." .

"And if a gentleman sitting in at a card party does nor appear to know his own name, it gives a bad impression."

"Precisely, monsieur."

James uttered his barking laugh and Roux started nervously.

"Tell me further," said James, "what were they going to pay you for your services?"

"Three thousand francs, monsieur."

"That does not seem to me to be very much, especially as I suppose you would be expected to furnish your aid if I were to prove recalcitrant?"

"Eh?"

"To resist."

Roux swallowed awkwardly and then said that a man was less likely to give trouble if there were three to one against him.

"That may well be. In any case, you do not seem very likely to draw your pay for tonight's work."

"No, monsieur."

"Particularly as we left them trying to murder each other. Charles, what think you?"

"Four thousand francs?" suggested Charles. James nodded and Charles tossed them across the table to Roux.

"Are these for me? Gentlemen," said Roux with apparently genuine emotion, "you are more than kind, you are generous. A thousand thanks."

"Four francs per thank, eh, James?"

"That is not quite the whole story," said James. "There is a little matter, Roux, in which we think you can help us."

"Anything I can do, gentlemen—"

"I take you to be a sharp fellow who knows his way about." Roux smiled. "We need a couple of passports, our hotel is dunning us for them."

"English passports?"

"Certainly—"

"One English and one American," said Charles firmly.

"Charles, as though it signified—"

"It does signify, Cousin. I am a Virginian and I will not sail under false colors."

"Oh, very well," said James. "I only thought that American passports might be more difficult to get; there cannot be so many Americans as English in Paris."

"The place is stiff with 'em," said Roux, staring. "There's nothing in it. English, American, whatever you wish."

"Then it can be done?"

"Certainly, monsieur. They will cost you five thousand francs each. I have a friend who is willing and able to oblige gentlemen who are in difficulties about passports."

"I thought you might have," said Charles.

"But will they be really good ones? We are not to be fobbed off with an inferior article."

"Monsieur, those which my friend produces would pass with Sir Eden himself."

"Look, Cousin," said Charles. "There is a small crowd interested in the hotel of our friends opposite."

James turned in his chair to look out of the window and Roux also leaned forward to see. There were, indeed, some twenty or thirty people gathered about the entrance; at the top of the half dozen steps which led up to the front door there stood a thin, worried-looking man gazing anxiously up and down the street.

"That man is, in fact, the proprietor," said Roux.

"Do you suppose that our friends, in their rage and despair, have set the hotel on fire?" said Charles.

"Let us wait," said James comfortably, "and see whether the fire brigade comes or the police."

Roux moved uneasily and Charles noticed it.

"Sir, I observe that the word 'police' appears to discompose you. May I opine, sir, that the relations between you and the police are something less than affable?"

Roux muttered something about a small misunderstanding, and the crowd parted to allow two *agents de police* in their neat blue uniforms to mount the steps to the front door. From the manager's gestures it was clear that there was some sort of trouble upstairs.

"Not fire," said James.

"Let us go, gentlemen," said Roux, rising to his feet. "I admit I do not care for the vicinity of the police, me."

"I think you are right," said Charles. "Not that the police make my head ache, but if those two are brought forth with ignominy and happened to sight us, they might accuse us of causing their woes."

"Let us summon a *fiacre*," said James, moving towards the door.

"Not that door," said Roux. "The other, in the side street. And not a *fiacre*, to the devil with them! A good swift taxi." He dodged out of the side door and the cousins followed him; a taxi providentially arrived and Roux, regardless of manners, leapt into it. The cousins exchanged glances and leisurely entered it after him.

"Where shall I tell the fellow to go?" asked Charles.

"Place de la Bastille, for a start," said Roux. "When we are there I will direct him."

He did so and they finally alighted in a road behind the Gare de Vincennes. Charles paid off the taxi and Roux led the way round two or three corners into a long, narrow, and ill-lit street.

"It was not worth while," said Roux carelessly, "letting that fellow know exactly where we were going."

"Reasonable precautions," said James, "are always to be commended."

"You make me feel like a conspirator," said Charles, bending down to speak in Roux's ear. "Are you conspiring anything?"

"Only to get your passports," said Roux, edging away. "This is the house. One moment."

He knocked at the door of a small shop where cheap stationery and magazines were for sale together with a very secondhand typewriter labeled "Bargain. 4500 frs." The shop was shut for the night, but shuffling footsteps approached it from inside, bolts were drawn, and an elderly man opened the door and peered out.

"Mosset, it's me, Roux. I have brought you two customers."

Mosset opened the door and asked them to come in; Roux went on ahead through the shop, but the cousins, stooping their heads under the low lintel, stood still until the door was fastened again.

"Please to go forward, gentlemen."

They went forward in the dim light and entered a lighted room at the back where Roux was already seated and glancing at a newspaper. Mosset, seen in the light, was a small man with a pleasant face and a neat gray beard. He looked up at the Latimers and appeared to like what he saw.

"What can I—" he began, but Roux, without looking up from the paper, interrupted him.

"Two passports, Mosset. One English, one American, and they'd better be good ones."

"If you please," finished Charles.

"I think I can manage that, gentlemen. Have you already got passport photographs?"

"Why, no," said James, looking startled. "Are they—We did not—"

Charles nudged him to be quiet. 'We reckoned we should do better to put the whole concern in your hands, Monsieur Mosset. Can you produce the whole thing, sir?"

"Certainly, gentlemen. We had better start with the photographs, if you will kindly come upstairs. You"—to Roux— "will stay here, will you not?"

Roux nodded and lit a cigarette while Mosset led the way up a steep and narrow flight of uncarpeted stairs. James and Charles Latimer put their hats down at the table behind Roux's chair before following; the moment they were out of sight Roux spun round and looked at the table. But Charles had taken his cardboard box with him.

Roux threw down the paper and relapsed into thought. That roll of notes was undoubtedly the same as that which Fosse and De Garth had lost, whatever the man called Charles might say to the contrary. It had been obtained by a trick, and men who could work tricks like that were worth cultivating. They had been generous to him; not that Roux was in the least grateful, but it did show a certain softness of disposition which might be turned to advantage. Most of Roux's acquaintances had dispositions which would cut grooves in a nether millstone; these two were different. Some sort of partnership, perhaps.

On the other hand, Roux had at least one good reason for wanting to leave Paris, a little matter of a dead Mexican who had gone into the Seine. Unfortunately the Seine had not retained him and he had come to lie, cold and dripping in an atmosphere of formalin, upon a slab in the morgue. Even that would not have mattered so much if the wretched corpse had not had a knife wound in the back. Roux did not know whether the police connected him with this affair, but one is never sure with the police. It would be better to leave Paris altogether for, say, Marseilles, provided one had a little nest egg to take with one. These Latimers' million francs, for example.

Roux sighed, threw away his cigarette butt, and lit another. If it were only the one who had been at the card party Roux would have felt more confident; it was the other, the tall one who appeared so inexplicably upon the hotel stairs, who made him nervous. For one thing, he was always laughing, and at what; It was not reassuring, that.

In the meantime, Charles and James were having their photographs taken and giving such particulars of themselves as passport offices rudely require. They filled up small forms under Mosset's direction. Their addresses: James gave his as Oakwood Hall, Didsbury, near Manchester, England, and Charles his as Oakwood, Shandon, Virginia, U.S.A. Dates of birth.

"August 11," said James, "let me see, now, I'm thirty-six, that makes it—"

"1917," said Mosset, and James wrote it down.

"You are six years my junior, Charles, are you not?"

"June 11," said Charles, counting rapidly in his head, "—er—1923. Yes, sir, I have the advantage of you by that amount."

"Occupations?" prompted Mosset.

"Mill owner," said James.

"Retired Army officer," said Charles.

"Just put 'retired,'" said Mosset. "Married?"

"Widower," said James.

"No," said Charles. "Why do they wish to know all these private matters?"

"The passport offices have not confided in me to that extent, gentlemen."

Charles smiled up at him as he bent over the table and James said that that would be all, with the signature, would it not?

"That is all, monsieur. That little form you have just filled in is itself stuck into the passport; that at least is perfectly genuine. Now for the photographs."

James was installed in a high-backed armchair and bright lights were turned upon him. Mosset brought out a large old-fashioned camera with a double-rack extension and retired behind it under a focusing cloth.

"How long do I have to keep still?" asked James.

"Only a moment, monsieur. One twenty-fifth of a second, to be exact, but I am not ready yet. I will tell you when the time comes."

James, who had already assumed the stern but noble expression he had worn for his portrait by Reinagle, R. A., in 1867, relaxed comfortably.

"Tell me, Monsieur Mosset," said Charles, "how did you come to take up this trade? For I cannot see you and doubt that you are an honest man; how come you to be the associate of such as that rogue downstairs?"

Mosset did not answer until he had the focus to his satisfaction, when he emerged from under the focusing cloth and said that Monsieur's penetrating courtesy touched him deeply. "But it is a mistake, monsieur, to assume that rogues live in a world apart and altogether set aside from honest men. They buy their stamps from honest postmasters and are shaved by honest barbers." He dived into his darkroom and came back with a dark slide in his hand.

"You, sir, are a philosopher," said Charles, sitting on the edge of a table and swinging his legs.

"No, monsieur, but I call myself honest because I work hard for my money and neither overcharge nor cheat. It is true that what I do is illegal, but a man must live. It is permissible, I hope, to distinguish between what is dishonest and what is merely illegal."

"Certainly," said Charles, "certainly."

"Besides, it is not for long. Near Dijon, monsieur, there is a vineyard and a little house; it is mine, it was my father's before me. It is not enough for a man to live on in the days of his strength, but to retire to, ah! The good God made it for that. I keep a bag packed, messieurs, and at the first sign of trouble with the police or with my neighbors, I pick up my bag and go. I have my own papers there and my own identity with which I was born; even my name is not Mosset there, I assumed it when I came to Paris. As for him whom Monsieur has so rightly described as 'that rogue downstairs,' he does but bring clients to me and get paid for doing so." He slid the dark slide into the camera. "One's firewood burns no less brightly for being brought in a filthy cart. Now, monsieur," to James, "if you are ready?"

He took two exposures and said that that would serve; the cousins changed places for Charles to face the camera while James nursed the cardboard box. Mosset, who seemed to like talking, said that it was seldom that he had clients of the stamp of those whom he now saw before him. Normally, persons who found themselves in difficulties with the passport authorities were either unhappy or—or—

"Scoundrelly," suggested Charles, and Mosset smiled.

"It always upsets me a little to make my livelihood out of the miseries of others," he said, fitting a fresh dark slide into the camera.

"You are wrong, sir," said Charles, "you should rejoice that you are able to help them. Do doctors hang their heads in shame because their customers are drawn only from the sick and suffering? No, sir, they rejoice, and so should you."

The corners of his long mouth curled up and his eyes filled with laughter; Mosset, who was watching his face, pressed the bulb of the shutter release.

"I will take another to make sure," he said, "but I think that one will be good. Steady a moment. Thank you."

James asked how soon the passports would be ready and Mosset said in an hour's time. There was the embossed stamp on the photograph to be done, and the rubber stamp of the port of entry. "Did you come by Calais, gentlemen? Or perhaps by air to Le Bourget? And the date?"

"Make it Calais, please," said James, "and date it a week ago. You will make flawless specimens, will you not? It would be most humiliating if the—"

"Monsieur need not be anxious and I will take extra care for the pleasure I have had in your company. One word of warning, if I do not presume——"

"Go on," said Charles.

"That man downstairs, how much do you know about him?"

"Trickster," said Charles. "Cardsharper. Probably a thief "

"He is worse than that," said Mosset. "He is dangerous. He is too quick with the knife, so they say."

"We shall get rid of him at once," said James. "Our only use for him was to bring us here."

"We are much in your debt," said Charles. "In an hour's time, then?"

They went downstairs and found Roux still sitting and reading the paper. James said, "Come," in a peremptory voice and Roux followed them meekly enough, for the cardboard box was still under Charles's arm. They went out into the street and Mosset bolted the door after them.

"We have an hour to wait," said James, looking discontentedly about him. "I suppose there is not even a reasonably passable café in these parts where gentlemen can sit for an hour and not be molested? Which is the way to the Place de la Bastille?"

"That is it," said Roux, pointing, "at the bottom of the street. There is a café there which I can recommend; it is simple indeed, but clean and well conducted. Let me show you."

He hurried along beside them; he had indeed almost to trot to keep up, for they made no attempt to suit their pace to a man eight inches shorter than they were. When they emerged upon the *place*, Roux said that that was the café in question, that one upon the opposite corner. He would be happy to take them in there; a word from him to the proprietor would ensure their receiving the most distinguished attention.

"Sure, sure," said Charles, beaming down upon him. "Nonetheless, we calculate we might go further and fare better, despite the proverb. Yes, sir, that is what we think. Cousin James, hail that taxi! Sir, though our acquaintance with you was unfortunate in the beginning, it has proved mutually profitable in the end, has it not: Sir, we part friends, I trust." The taxi whirled to a stop and James stepped in. "Adieu, sir," added Charles, pressing a note into Roux's hand, "remember us in your prayers. The Rotonde at Montparnasse, driver, please." The door slammed behind him and they drove away.

"Ditched," said Roux with an oath, "ditched. Well, that settles it." He unfolded the note in his palm; it was to the value of one hundred francs, about two shillings.

CHAPTER X:
Roux Dances

THE LATIMERS came back to the Bastille area an hour later to receive their passports and took a little trouble to reach Mosset's house by a different route. By that time it was well past midnight and the sordid streets were even darker and more sinister than they had been earlier. There were but few people about, and such as were slunk or scuttled like rats in the shadows. Across the road from Mosset's house two men were lounging in an entry, big young men with caps pulled over their eyes and mufflers round their necks.

"Friends of Roux; What say you, Charles?"

"I am of your opinion, James. Else, why watch Mosset's door? I do not see Roux— Yes, there he is."

"I see him. Within that further doorway; he looked out and then withdrew his head. Now, if Mosset delays to open the door—"

But Mosset must have been watching for them from within the darkened shop, for they heard bolts being withdrawn as they approached and the door opened as they reached it.

"Come in, gentlemen, quickly." Mosset seemed nervous, for the bolts rattled in his hand as he shot them home. "I wish now that I had told you to come back in the morning; there is something stirring in this quarter tonight and it alarms me."

"Indeed?" said James. "What sort of a stir?"

"My old housekeeper came in half an hour ago and begged me not to go out on any account and not to open my door until I had seen who was outside. There is some rumor of someone carrying a lot of money who is to be relieved of it."

"So long as they do not relieve me of my new shoes," laughed Charles, tapping his cardboard box.

"Also, Roux is back. I saw him ten minutes ago speaking with those two men in the entry opposite— Ah, they are gone now. They are bad types, those two, Bibi le Vaseux and Collet-serré. Never mind, let us go upstairs."

In one respect at least Roux had spoken the truth, for the passports were such as any Foreign Office would have been proud to own.

"The photographs, too," said Mosset, "I am pleased with the photographs. Yours, Monsieur James Latimer, is the portrait of an *homme au grand seriéux,* and yours, Monsieur Charles, when one looks it is about to speak. They are too good for passports, I who made them say it."

They paid him what he asked and a couple of thousand francs over,

since he admitted that that was what he would have to pay Roux for
introducing them, and then took their leave. Mosset came down to open
the door for them and peered anxiously out of the shopwindow.

"I cannot see anyone about," he said, "but I do not like your going
out. This is a poor hovel, but will you not stay here till morning? There
is a couch——"

They laughed at his fears. "I will fight for my new shoes," said Charles,
hugging his box, "like the savagest tiger in the Bois, and when I have
torn my assailants to shreds my cousin will stamp upon the quivering
morsels. Sir, you do not know us."

But Mosset was not reassured. "Wait here a moment while I open
the door and look up and down the street. No. No, I see no one. Walk
quickly, gentlemen, in the middle of the road, and if anyone comes out
of the shadows, run, for the love of heaven, run!"

They shook him by the hand and went out; as the door closed behind them Mosset's anxious whisper floated after them: "Remember,
gentlemen, run!"

They walked on quickly down the middle of the road towards the
Place de la Bastille and Charles glanced over his shoulder.

"They are coming, Cousin," he said. "Oily Bibi on one side and
Tight-collar upon the other. Roux is not far behind."

"He is afraid they will snatch your box and run and he will never see
it again," said James calmly. "I take it the gentleman called Tight-collar
is a garrotter?"

"No doubt, Cousin, no doubt. Do we run?"

"No," said James. "It would not be dignified; besides, they might
run faster than we. Let us puzzle them instead. Wait until they are upon
us."

Bibi le Vaseux was armed with a blackjack, which is a short club
loaded with lead, and Collet-serré held a short length of cord in both
hands. They crept up close behind the Latimers; Collet-serré lifted both
hands with the cord between them, Bibi le Vaseux swung up his blackjack and brought it down on the head of James Latimer——

But there was nothing there and the blackjack proceeded through
the arc of its travel and struck its owner heavily upon the kneecap. Such
a blow is agonizingly painful; Bibi gave one awful yell and dropped his
weapon to clutch his knee with both hands.

Collet-serré was unhurt physically but even more frightened; he had
been brought up in pious circles and still believed in the devil. He had
felt the strangling cord touch upon the brim of Charles's hat and then
there was no one there. He uttered a whine of terror and ran like a
startled cat, with Bibi leaping and hopping after him, still clasping his

cracked kneecap but making very good speed for all that, almost as good as Collet-serré's, whose legs were weak with fear.

Doors opened at the sound of Bibi's yell and dark entries filled with gaping faces, for Mosset's housekeeper was right, the rumor had gone round and the quarter was awake. But no one came out to help them and no voice called to them to "turn in here," for if they had bungled an affair they must take the consequences. Besides, there was something else for the onlookers to see.

Roux came down the road, following his friends. He appeared to be quite alone and he was dancing wildly. He ran, and his feet hardly touched the ground; he leapt, and the great Nijinsky himself never bounded as Roux did. His arms were held out stiffly in line with his shoulders, with the elbows bent as in Russian traditional dances; his legs were going all ways at once; his face was a mask of terror and as he went he cried, "Help! Help!" at one moment and "No, no, let me go!" the next. At one moment he revolved slowly as in some stately pavane, at another he sprang forward suddenly as does one who is vulgarly urged from behind. He zigzagged across the road and leapt in the air at every turn; one would say he had imperfectly studied the graceful *can-can*. At one point he seemed to be trying to bite his right shoulder, and at that his legs flew up in the air and he sat down with an audible thud, only to bounce like an india rubber ball. He curvetted like a frisky pony and pranced like a turkey-cock among his hens; he appeared to be trying to butt sideways with his head and the next moment he shook all over, not as a man shivers with fever but as a sail shakes when the helmsman puts the boat about, and his head wobbled upon his shoulders. Bibi le Vaseux and Collet-serré paused in their flight at the sound of his cries; when they looked back and saw him bounding after them like a galloping horse, eight feet to the bound, they yelled with terror and fled faster than before, and Roux gamboled after them.

"He is smitten with madness!" muttered the watchers in the door-ways.

"He is drunk, that's all."

"Drunk? What drink ever turned a man into a kangaroo?"

"See his legs go round in the air? One would say he is riding an invisible bicycle."

"He has the St. Vitus' dance. He should be caught and taken to hospital."

"His clothes are full of wasps, I can hear them."

"You are all wrong," said an old woman, crossing herself incessantly, "it is his sins which have taken hold upon him. See, they are shaking him like a blanket."

"It is a judgment we are seeing——"

The procession emerged upon the Place de la Bastille and the policeman on traffic duty turned in astonishment as Collet-serré, sobbing with fright, and Bibi, still holding one leg and leaping with the other, passed him by. Then Roux emerged into the lights. He sailed through the air towards the policeman, landed with a jolt which rattled his teeth, and passed on, leaning forward at an angle of forty-five with his toes trailing. Another spasm brought him to his feet again and he went on in a series of short hops like a frog.

The policeman stared after him. There was always some devilry going on in this quarter, usually directed against the police. He hesitated, twirling his truncheon. It was inadvisable to let oneself be made a fool of, one's sergeant would not be sympathetic. It is not a crime to dance along the street. He returned to his duty.

Bibi le Vaseux and Collet-serré ran down side turnings and disappeared from sight, but Roux pursued his eccentric course towards the nearest police station. When it became evident where he was going, the little crowd which was running beside him slowed up and fell back.

"*A moi! A moi!*" wailed Roux. "*Au secours*—help! A rescue, a rescue!"

One man ran towards him with arms outstretched, but Roux's legs flew up to kick him in the stomach and he drew back discomfited.

"If that's what you does——"

Within the police station a pale young clerk sat at a table in the corner making entries in ledgers while the desk sergeant sat, solid and imperturbable, in the swivel chair behind his big desk. Outside the door there was a cry of despair and Roux burst in. He capered towards the sergeant, executed a gesture of greeting which was more like a curtsey than a bow, and waltzed past the desk towards the passage leading to the cells. In the doorway he paused, waggled a limp hand at the end of a stiff arm, and sprang forward out of sight. There came the iron clang of a cell door closing.

"What the——" said the sergeant, rising slowly to his feet. "What the—— I suppose he's drunk."

The outer door opened again and the constable who had been on traffic duty in the Place de la Bastille came in, for he had just been relieved.

"Did you see that fellow who has just come in?" asked the sergeant.

"Was he dancing?" asked the policeman cautiously.

"I suppose you could call it that," said the sergeant, taking a bunch of keys from a drawer. "He seems to have locked himself in one of the cells. Come with me."

They went along the passage. Since no prisoners had been brought

"I don't know what I do want," said the man frankly, "but this is Paris and I guess I want something that couldn't happen anyplace else."

They went up to the Butte Montmartre and sat on hard benches in a dark ancient room to listen to those light and charming little songs which the French alone seem able to compose and sing. There was a violinist also who set their feet tapping, and Charles discovered that he liked cherry brandy. When they came out from there he encountered the American again.

"Well, sir? I trust that that was more in your humor?"

"Mighty fine," said the American gloomily, "mighty fine. But I was thinking as we drove up here, when I could stop saying my prayers on some of those corners—I'll say our driver can drive—I was thinking that the word to describe what I'm looking for is sinister. Yes, sir, dark alleys with lurking figures and an atmosphere of nameless evil is what I had in mind."

Charles thought of Collet-serré and laughed, but James was rather shocked. He said a little severely that a party which included ladies could not possibly be exposed to contact with depravity.

"Why, no, sir, no. I was not unmindful of the ladies in the party, but couldn't somebody just draw me aside and tell me about it quietly?"

Then they were once more on the road; their guide rose and said that the next place to which they were bound was of great historic interest, being established in the dungeons of one of the most notorious prisons of Paris in the days of the Terror and for centuries before.

"I had, perhaps, better warn the ladies that the decor is designed to startle and that no attempt has been made to soften the grimness of the place. There is also a full-sized guillotine there which you will see in operation." Small squeaks from some of the ladies, but not from Dorothy or Maud. "I need hardly say that the performance is a very clever trick, but it is certainly impressive, and there is no question about the genuineness of the surroundings." Charles glanced across at the American, who gestured with a lifted thumb. "After that, the rest of the evening will be spent at the Bal Tabarin, which I am sure you will all enjoy. Thank you very much."

They disembarked in a dark street, entered a low doorway, and immediately descended a long flight of steep irregular stairs, plainly very old, most of which seemed to be cut from the solid rock.

"This, sir, seems to be more to your liking," said Charles to the American.

"Yes, sir. Yes," as they reached the perfectly genuine dungeons at the bottom, "I guess if these walls could speak the ladies had better not listen. No, sir."

They passed into a long narrow room furnished with pitchpine pews such as are, or used to be, found in chapels of the less Sybaritic orders; the shelf along the back of each pew, which, in the prototype, is provided for hymn books and Bibles, is here adapted to hold glasses. There is a stage at the far end upon which is set a full-sized guillotine. It is a startling sight, especially as the board below the hole through which the victim's head emerges is liberally daubed and dripping with red paint of exactly the right color. The only departure from precedent is that the board, to which the victim's body is normally strapped, is replaced by a chair.

"Gruesome," said Dorothy. "Macabre."

"In the true Grand Guignol tradition," said Maud. "Very French." They filed into one of the pews and James followed them in, with Charles next him at the end.

"Let us pray," said another of the English contingent in a strong Lancastrian accent, and laughed loudly. Dorothy said, "Oh, really," in a low voice, Maud looked down her nose, and James said that the remark was, indeed, not in the best taste.

"One is rather apt, on these tours," said Maud to James, "to find oneself in rather mixed company."

"Very true, ma'am, very true. Yet, if one takes pleasure in travel, the risk has to be taken. But, on the whole, our companions are sufficiently well behaved."

Dorothy, who did not see why Maud should have the more than personable James all to herself, leaned across and said that no doubt the guide would be able to deal with any marked irregularity of conduct in the party and James agreed. Waitresses, dressed in the costume of the women of the Terror, came round with trays of glasses filled with red wine and the performance began with a display of really first-class conjuring, especially considering that the conjurer was practically on top of his audience. Perhaps the highest spot of this performance was a trick in which the conjurer put a pack of cards into a tumbler, held it up, and asked any member of the audience to call for whatever card he wished. The name card could then be seen to extricate itself from the pack and crawl slowly out of the tumbler. Well-deserved applause followed.

Maud said something inaudible to Dorothy, who replied, "Why not ask your friend next you?"

"Ma'am, is there any matter in which I can be of service? Pray command me."

Maud looked faintly surprised but said, "It was only—I was wondering whether they would be hurt if I did not drink my wine?"

"You do not care for it? Pray let me—"

"No, no, please. It is only that I am not much of a toper—ha, ha!—and I would really rather not have any more just at present."

"Besides," said Dorothy, leaning forward, "there will be champagne at the Bal Tabarin, I believe."

"Leave it, ma'am, just leave it. When we go, no one will know which of the party did not drink their wine."

"That is perfectly true. Thank you." Maud pushed her glass back on the shelf and settled herself to watch the entertainer. He had set back his little table to the side of the stage out of his way and was introducing the guillotine. He said it was a real one, a very good one, and it worked. He hauled up the heavy knife to the top of the slide, placed a large potato in the exact spot where the victim's neck would be, and pulled the lever. The knife flashed down with a dull thud at the bottom and the potato fell into two pieces, which were shown to the audience. Positively no deception, ladies and gentlemen. Swift, painless, and effective.. All one's troubles ended at a stroke. Would any gentleman care to come and have his troubles ended? Ah, come on. Surely, among the distinguished company present there must be one hero who was prepared to make so small a sacrifice to round off the evening's amusement? *Allons, mes braves!*

Charles rose to his feet and walked up to the stage to the applause of the company. He carried a glass of wine in his hand and James watched him with some apprehension, for it was the second glass he had had there besides what had been supplied earlier in the evening. Charles never got drunk but he did tend to become carefree and even reckless as the drinks wore on. A certain lack of discretion—

"Your friend is a brave man," said Maud with a laugh.

"My cousin, ma'am, is one who always finds it impossible to refuse a challenge."

"But there is no real risk, surely," said Dorothy.

"None, ma'am, positively none at all."

Charles stepped upon the stage, put his glass of wine down on the conjurer's little table, and walked to the guillotine.

"I am your executioner, I am 'Monsieur de Paris,' " said the entertainer. "Please to sit on this chair. Let me draw it up close, there, now. Before I operate, may I ask if you have made your will? All your final dispositions settled? Excellent, excellent. No last messages for loving friends at home, eh? Splendid, splendid. Now, if you will kindly put your head through this hole, as so many of the gallant and gay have done before you—face downwards, if you please. A little further in—thank you. Now then. One moment while I fetch the basket—"

The traditional basket, with sawdust in it to catch the head and other by-products of decapitation, was put down in front of the guillotine. Charles, rather uncomfortably posed with his neck stretched out and his head through the hole, looked down into the basket and then screwed his face round to laugh at the audience. The man was by the lever, but there seemed to be rather a long pause.

Charles twisted his head round to see what was happening and saw the conjurer apparently turned to stone. He had his hand on the lever but he was staring past the guillotine at his little table. Charles managed to look that way also, and at that moment the audience saw it too, for there was an outbreak of ahs and squeals of laughter.

There was a small brown monkey sitting on the table with Charles's wineglass in both hands and he was drinking the wine with every appearance of delight.

The conjurer jerked the lever, the knife fell with the usual sickening thud, and Charles Latimer completely vanished. There was no body on the chair, no head in the basket, and, what was more, no red-coated monkey on the table.

The conjurer clung to the guillotine, for his knees were giving way. The audience gasped and then a babble of cries broke out.

"Where's he gone? How's it done? Where's the monkey? How's it done? Damned clever!" Some of them turned white and rose to go; others, whose sight was perhaps no longer so clear as it had been earlier in the evening, applauded wildly. "Damned good show! Encore! Encore!"

"Sir," said Dorothy in a shaking voice, "how in the name of goodness did your cousin do that?"

James pulled himself together. "All prearranged, ma'am. My cousin knows the conjurer. Little matter of trap doors— black velvet curtains— all that sort of thing. Ha, ha! Clever, is it not? I do not myself, ma'am, know the details, but my cousin was ever a merry-andrew. Never know what he will be at——"

He was interrupted by a nudge at his side and a barely suppressed scream from Maud, who slid along the bench away from him.

"That monkey again!"

Ulysses was standing on the bench between them, his cap over one eye and his jacket unbuttoned, stretching out a not too steady hand towards Maud's discarded wine. James ejaculated, "Get away!" and aimed a slap at him; the monkey ran past him and appeared to leap into the air and vanish, though as by then most of the company were standing up and filling the aisles it was difficult to say where he went.

"This," said Maud, "is, quite without exception, the cleverest performance I have ever seen anywhere. Almost too good, if you know what

I mean?"

"Perhaps," said Dorothy, "the performance at the Bal Tabarin will be a little more restful, do you think?"

The company filed out, with compliments to the manager. They did not see the conjurer; he was in a little room at the back, being revived with brandy.

The guide, who had really been upset by the guillotine episode but who had trained himself not to show his emotions, came up to James while the party was re-embarking.

"The gentleman who was with you, I don't see him. Has he gone off somewhere—had we better wait for him?"

"No, no. On no account delay the tour. He knows Paris quite well and is perfectly capable of looking after himself."

"I am sure he is," said the guide with some emphasis.

"Pray continue with the tour. I dare say that he will rejoin us later."

At the Bal Tabarin the guide assembled his party together and said, "Tables have been reserved for us, ladies and gentlemen. Please follow me closely." He led the way in and they all trooped after him; as soon as they were inside James saw him check suddenly and his shoulders stiffened. Charles was there already, leaning gracefully against a pillar, watching the dancing which takes place on the floor while the stage is curtained for the interval. He looked round and saw them; his face lit up and he waved his cigar in greeting.

"I missed you at the last stop," he said genially. "I must have come out by the wrong door, or some such, so I stole a march upon you, as you see."

"You were very quick," said the guide.

"Why not?" said Charles's American friend just behind the guide. "Sure, sure, the world's divided between the quick and the dead and, there's no doubt which you are."

"Say you so," said Charles, beaming upon him.

"That disappearing act of yours was just the very finest illusion I've ever seen put over. You're a real smart guy if you will let me say so, but how the devil did you work it?"

"That is a secret between me and the conjurer," said Charles darkly. "You will not expect me to give away professional secrets?"

"Why, no, but——"

"Take your seats, please," said the guide.

"That is what you told us," said Dorothy to James, but smiling at Charles, "though I still cannot see how it was done."

"If you could, ma'am," said Charles, "it would not be much of a mystery, would it?"

"Please sit down," said the guide patiently. "Any of these vacant tables here."

They were small tables, each with four chairs round them and each with four bottles of champagne, two by two in ice pails.

"Pray, ladies," said James, "where will you please to sit? Here? Allow me—"

He and Charles drew out the ladies' chairs, hovered politely until they were comfortable, and then begged leave to sit at the same table. The leave was all the more willingly granted because Dorothy and Maud, who were quite human in spite of having been extremely well brought up, were happily aware of envious glances from younger and smarter women in the party. Attentive waiters rushed round opening bottles and gentle pops filled the air. James half rose in his chair, glass in hand. "Ladies, your very good health." Charles followed suit, bowing to each of them separately.

"Ma'am. Ma'am. Your bright eyes." He drained his glass and refilled it. A gong sounded, the floor cleared of dancers, and the gray velvet curtains slid back from the stage.

They sat and watched, entranced, what is admittedly the finest stage spectacle to be seen anywhere in the world. They talked little since there was so much to see, but James noticed uneasily that Charles had finished his own bottle and had started upon James's and that his face was alight with mischief. Heaven alone knew what would happen if his demon impelled him to join the trampoline act on the stage.

As though the thought had communicated itself to Charles, he said: "How wonderful, Cousin James, to bound like that upon spring mattresses and fly through the air. Look, two somersaults! I am sure one could do three."

James intervened. "Cousin, a word with you apart. Ladies, if your goodness will excuse us for a brief moment? Some tiresome but urgent business I have just remembered—"

"Must you, James, just at this moment?"

"Pray, Charles, humor me so far."

"Oh, very well!"

"Ladies, a moment only—"

"And not a moment longer than I can help," said Charles gallantly, and followed his cousin to one of the side bars which happened to be empty except for the barmaid.

"Charles! Pray bear with me while I beg you to behave with more decorum. No indeed, it will not do. You are drinking more than you realize, and such a variety of drinks is most insidious."

"My dear good elder cousin—"

"Charles, please! Pray do not take it amiss—"

Charles burst out laughing and threw his arm round his cousin's shoulder. "Dear James, you are in the right, as always. I am perhaps getting a little elevated, but what fun this evening has been! I will be good, I will not join the trampoline act upon the stage, much as I should like to. Talking about stages—"

"You spoiled that unfortunate conjurer's act for him—"

"Oh no!"

"And frightened him nearly to death."

"He did turn a little green," said Charles thoughtfully, "but I think that was Ulysses' intervention, was it not?"

"No," said James firmly, "for Ulysses might conceivably have got in somehow, but for your disappearance there was no accounting at all."

"True. True. I ought to make some sort of reparation, ought I not?"

"Charles, what a good fellow you are," said James, melting suddenly. "I lecture you like some stuffy pedagogue and your sweet temper takes it all in good part."

"It is my sweet common sense which tells me that you are justified," said Charles. "May I have one more before I go? Mademoiselle, a little glass of—what shall I have?"

"Champagne, monsieur?"

"Two glasses, please. Thank you. To your bright eyes!"

The girl giggled archly and turned away for a moment to bring down some more glasses from an upper shelf. When she looked round again Charles's glass was empty and he had gone. She uttered a tiny scream.

"The monsieur! Where has he gone?"

"Elsewhere, mademoiselle, elsewhere," said James, drinking slowly. "This is very good wine."

"But so quick!" said the girl, not to be diverted. "It is like magic! He is there, I look away for a second, and poof! he is gone!"

"How much do I owe you?" said James.

He returned to the table and to his deserted ladies and made excuses for Charles's absence. "My cousin instructed me to make his humble apologies, he has been detained, he will return as soon as possible."

"It is a pity that he should miss anything of this wonderful show," said Dorothy. "Look, do you see that girl in blue? She fascinates me— wait till she turns—there! She has a mask on the back of her head, an exact copy of her own face, it is uncanny."

"She keeps her own face so still," said James, "it is masklike in itself."

"How pretty she is!" said Maud.

Some time passed before James heard a burst of laughter from one of the other tables where four young women were sitting together. He looked round and saw Charles swaying slightly on his feet and smiling down on them; on his shoulder sat a small brown monkey who bowed and took off his cap. James got up with a word of apology and went towards him just as one of the girls handed him a full glass. Charles raised it to each of them in turn.

"Ladies. To your bright eyes!"

CHAPTER XII
Nice Women

BEFORE JAMES LATIMER, sidling between close-packed tables, could reach his cousin's side the manager of the Bal Tabarin was there, having been sent for in haste.

"Monsieur, I am completely desolated to interrupt your enjoyment, but to bring animal pets into the Bal Tabarin definitely cannot be permitted."

One of the girls intervened with a loud titter. "But he's so sweet!"

Charles turned slowly to face the manager. "Sir, my monkey is well trained. I will go bail for his good behavior under the most trying circumstances. Indeed, sir, he is not what you think."

"Monsieur, I have no doubt but that your pet is a monkey of the most unrivalled excellence. Nonetheless, if he is allowed to remain, other patrons will think themselves entitled to bring other animals of a baser sort. Consider, monsieur, the effect upon our elaborate spectacles of an irruption upon the stage of excited dogs, dissolute cats, and unbridled monkeys. Sir, if our poor show has pleased you at all, I beg you to have mercy upon it."

Charles, who was beginning to turn obstinate, suddenly relaxed into peals of laughter so infectious that even the anxious manager joined in. "Dissolute cats! Sir, what a shocking suggestion. The picture you call up—gentlemen, hush! Dissolute cats—Ulysses, let us go, 'lest one good custom should corrupt the world.' " He turned to go, with the relieved manager at his elbow, and noticed the small bar which he and James had visited before. "Sir, with your good leave, may my little friend have one last nightcap?"

The manager agreed rather unwillingly; Charles swept him into the bar and ordered drinks for all three—"A small glass of port for my little friend. He should not take wine in excess." The barmaid took the strain admirably and when Ulysses stood upon the bar, took his cap right off, and bowed low, hand on heart, first to her and then to the manager, he said that Monsieur's little creature was certainly a monkey of the utmost decorum. James hovered in the background, not willing to interfere while everything was going well.

"Drink up your wine, Ulysses, it is time for bed. Dissolute cats!"

Their guide was sitting in a corner of the bar together with the guide of the next party which had followed theirs upon almost exactly the same round. They were old friends, they had been comparing notes upon the evening's events, and they were both watching Charles and his monkey with an unwinking stare.

Ulysses finished his wine and set down the empty glass. Charles did not notice, for he was watching the stage, and there was a short silence which the manager broke.

"Thank you, monsieur, for your kind hospitality. I hope that we shall often see you here again. And now you will take your charming pet home, will you not?"

"No need," said Charles carelessly, " he can perfectly well go home by himself. Yes, sir, I am mighty proud to show you this is no ordinary monkey." He waved his hand gracefully two or three times over Ulysses' head. "Hey, presto! Home, Ulysses."

Ulysses became a monkey-shaped shimmer, as it were, hung in the air for a second, and vanished completely.

"There, sir," said Charles, taking the manager's arm. "Dissolute cats! Are you satisfied now? Let us return to the ladies 'whose bright eyes rain favors and—' "

He was interrupted by the barmaid, whose loud scream faltered in mid-yell, fell to a wail, and stopped as she slid gracefully to the floor. At the end of the bar the two guides were clinging frantically together and unashamedly trying to hide their faces on each other's shoulder. People in the audience were looking round and the manager was justifiably furious.

"Really, sir, this is unpardonable! How dare you cause these scenes here? Will you have the goodness to leave at once or must I take further measures?"

"Pray, sir, calm yourself—"

"I will not! I am responsible for—"

"Hush," said Charles, "you are alarming the ladies. Do you wish to disappear also?" He stretched himself to his full six foot three and waved his hand majestically over the manager's head.

"No, no! Monsieur is undoubtedly a great magician—"

Charles tucked the manager's arm comfortably under his own and turned him towards the auditorium.

"Pray, sir, listen. You have seen nothing extraordinary, believe me.

No, sir, and I will prove it. You know that motorcar wheels have spokes?"

"Motorcar wheels have spokes," repeated the manager in a dazed voice.

"But when the motorcar is traveling along and the wheels are revolving rapidly, do you see the spokes?"

"See the spokes? No."

"But they are there all the time. It is your eyesight which is deficient. Is it not?"

"Is it not," agreed the manager.

"Precisely," said Charles happily. "Now let us rejoin the ladies." He led him firmly out of the bar.

"But," said the manager, jibbing, "that being the case, where is the monkey?"

"Gone home," said Charles, and smiled angelically.

James heard the rest of the story in the morning, over breakfast.

"I went back to the guillotine place," said Charles, "and found my poor friend the conjurer going through his performance again for the benefit of another group of tourists. 'Pon my honor, James, I thought at first that it was the same group and that my going on to the Bal Tabarin and seeing you all come in had been a dream. Cousin James, are all these parties exactly alike? There were even two Englishwomen like our Dorothy and our Maud, and four girls in a group who giggled, and a tall American—"

"But not, I venture to assert, two men like us."

"Well, no. No, sir, I allow that that is a well-founded statement. But stay, Cousin. Suppose that there are other men—and women—in all respects like us walking about in this world, should we be aware of it? Would some inner prompting tell us—"

"I would prefer you to tell me what happened last night."

"Dear James! Well, I stood back and did not show myself to begin with. He had just finished slicing the potato and was trying to persuade some hero to come up and be decapitated, but no one wished to offer himself. He said that upon the last occasion when he had done this trick the gentleman had been so startled that he had vanished into thin air. The conjurer said that he could not promise to do this again but he would try to if anyone would—no? He said, 'If I were a great magician I would bring the gentleman back. I would wave my arms thus, saying, "Hey, presto!" and there he would be.' Well, naturally, there I was."

"Charles, you will kill the fellow with fright."

"On the contrary, Cousin, it went down very well. No, sir, the fellow was not frightened. To speak by the book, he had been fortifying himself with strong drink and he took me in his stride."

"And the audience?"

"I will allow, James, that they gasped for air, but I believe the sensation to have been pleasurable."

"The ladies did not swoon? Charles, Charles, you would carry off a murder, upon my soul."

"No lady swooned. I sat down again upon the fatal chair and put my head through that infernal hole. He pulled the lever, the knife came down, and I withdrew myself all in one piece to general applause. Cousin, I behaved impeccably, 'pon my honor."

"I am assured of it and delighted to hear that all ended so well."

"It did not quite end there," said Charles a little hesitantly, "but indeed it was not my fault. I was about to leave the place with the rest of the tourists when the conjurer seized upon me. He wanted a word with me, and since he held me firmly by the arm I thought it better to accede gracefully. He led me to the bar. By this time, you understand, the place was empty except for the manager counting money somewhere in the background, the bartender collecting glasses from the pews, the conjurer, and myself. He desired me earnestly to go into partnership with him."

"Really, Charles!"

"Oh, believe me, Cousin, he meant no offense. He said that I was a conjurer of the first order and probably a Grand Master of the Magician's Circle—I hope I have it right. He said he had no idea how I did it—I did not enlighten him. He said that if he and I could work together we should sweep the halls."

"My dear Charles! Are you sure he said that?"

"I asked him to repeat it. Then I said that surely there would be servants of the lower sort to do that and he roared with laughter and said I was a star."

"Star," said James thoughtfully. "I have heard that term applied to a stage performer."

"Then he gave me a drink. Cousin James, I ask you quite seriously whether you have ever heard of Calvados."

"Certainly," said James promptly. "It is a department of France in the province of Normandy. I have—I had—a correspondent there."

"One does not drink a department of France. I asked what it was— I was already beginning to feel that a little more would be too much— and he said that it was a harmless beverage derived from the juice of apples." Charles sighed and passed a hand across his brow. "I allow it may have been made from the juice of apples. He went on talking; I remember his saying that with me as partner he would be taken on at the Bal Tabarin. Such, it appears, is his ambition. I refused. I said that I was a lecturer in hydrodynamics at the University of Virginia and I must return to my post. He said we should make more money in a week 'on the halls' than I should in a month as a stuffy university professor. I said I was not interested in money and he asked me if there were any insanity in my family."

James made shocked noises, but Charles proceeded. "By this time I was prepared to believe that there was and that I was its victim. That Calvados—however. The bartender had come back to the bar by this time and he and the conjurer were drinking Dubonnet. You remember the stuff we thought was a medicine? We were wrong, it is a blended liquor of some sort, dark red and served in small glasses. Naturally, Ulysses thought it was port, but I opine that the taste is very different. There was a loud spluttering noise, a yelp from the bartender, Dubonnet spraying all over the place, and Ulysses on my shoulder chattering with disgust. The conjurer said it was illusion and the bartender said it was the devil. So I said good night and came away."

"Came away?"

"Walked off up the stairs and into the street like anyone else. There was yet another party in the act of arriving, so the conjurer could not pursue me. James, I admit with shame that the latter period of our visit to the Bal Tabarin is by no means clear in my recollection. I trust I said and did nothing to alarm the ladies?"

"On the contrary," said James with a twinkle in his eyes. "You told Miss Maud that her eyes were like irises overhanging a dark pool and Miss Dorothy that her left eyebrow had exactly the sweep of a seraph's wing."

Charles hid his face in his hands.

"Then you asked where they were staying," pursued James, "and they said that it was not worth your while to know as they were leaving for England early today."

"Bless their stout sensible shoes," murmured Charles, "may they live happily ever after. Nice women."

"There is quite a long account in this newspaper," said James Latimer, "of the magistrate's examination of that fellow Roux. He is charged with the murder, by stabbing, of a Mexican whose body was taken up from the Seine."

"Indeed," said Charles, letting his long form down by degrees into an armchair in the De Bussy lounge. "We said, in our little note to the police, that we believed they wanted him, but I for one did not realize how badly."

"Mosset, the photographer, said that Roux was too ready with his knife," said James, passing the paper to his cousin; "it seems that he was

CHAPTER XIII:
Ointment for Bruises

IT WAS TOWARDS four o'clock of a hot and heavy afternoon; Paris was banking up for one of her far too numerous thunderstorms and the air was humid and oppressive. Inside the police station the pale clerk was drooping dispiritedly over his ledgers and the desk sergeant was frankly dozing in his chair. Within one of the four cells François Mosset sat hunched upon his bed, trying vainly to think up some reasonably credible explanation for no less than eleven passports in various stages of alteration. The police had them now, but they had been in his chest of drawers, under his shirts.

The cell door opened quietly and Mosset looked up, but the face which smiled at him, finger to lip, round the door was Charles Latimer's, not the sergeant's. Charles whispered, "Sh-sh! Not a sound! We have come to get you out." He entered the cell, closely followed by James.

"We have arranged it all," murmured James. "We have borrowed some American clothes for you, an American valise, and even—"

Mosset's gray beard drooped with surprise.

"A—excuse me—"

"An American suitcase," said the more modern-minded Charles, "plastered all over, sir, with hotel labels. You will not object, sir, to cutting off your beard?"

"Monsieur, to get myself out of this embroilment I would even cut off one hand!"

Charles explained that all Mosset had to do was to run through the charge-room and out into the street where Collet-serré would be waiting to pilot him, still at the gallop, to Bibi le Vaseux's room, where he could shave and change. After that a taxi to the Gare de Lyon and a seat in the five o'clock train to Dijon.

"B-but, messieurs, you are mad! Quite mad. Those two murderous villains will instantly betray us to the police—not only me, but you also—you cannot trust them."

"We do not have to trust them. We have a hold over them which they dare not even try to break. They are terrified of us, Mosset, and rightly. Their very lives are in our hands."

"Oh—in that case it is different. What do you wish me to do?"

The sky darkened over Paris and the oppression increased. The clerk abandoned his ledgers and lost himself in a half-waking dream of a new bicycle; a racing machine, naturally, with a high saddle, dropped handlebars, and a fixed gear. Very light and strong. Scarlet or electric blue? He gazed vacantly before him. A figure came to the end of the passage leading from the cells and paused there, but the clerk did not look round. The figure was abruptly projected forward as though pushed from behind; at that moment the sergeant's head fell forward, he uttered a loud snort and woke himself up. He opened his eyes just in time to see his prisoner running like a hare through the charge-room, past the clerk's desk and out at the door.

The sergeant sprang up with a bellow of rage and rushed at the door just as the clerk also leapt from his seat. They met in the doorway, impeding each other. In the struggle the sergeant caught his foot in the doormat and fell with a crash, bearing down with him the fragile form of the clerk as a felled oak will crush to the ground any spindling tree which may stand in the path of its fall. The sergeant scrambled hastily to his feet.

"All stations call—prisoner escaped," he said, and ran out into the street in time to see François Mosset disappearing round the corner at which Collet-serré, already out of sight, had been waiting for him. But the sergeant must have been more shaken by his fall than he realized, for before he had run twenty yards he tripped and fell again, heavily enough to wind himself. He sat up, crowing, gasping, and shaking his head, for there was no one near him except three small children loudly hushing each other, the sergeant was resting himself. There was no one near and yet he had fallen over an outstretched human leg, not a child's but a man's. He got up stiffly and returned to the police station.

Here he found his clerk sitting against the front edge of the sergeant's desk, telephoning the sad news of the escape and tenderly caressing his left ear, which had rudely collided with the doorpost. The clerk had his back to the desk; as the sergeant drew near, it seemed to him that there was something on it which had not been there when he left it.

There were some French currency notes and a message, written in the same pointed hand as the previous message, upon the back of a used envelope.

"We gave you Roux so we have taken Mosset. Our apologies for defacing your charge-book before. Ointment for bruises herewith."

The "ointment" was three thousand francs. The sergeant picked them up quickly and stuffed them into a drawer; the envelope he put carefully away into an inside pocket to be burned when he reached home. Then he sat down and took his head in his hands. The clerk finished telephoning and returned to his place without so much as a glance at the sergeant's desk.

"Pierre! Did anyone come in while I was out?"

"No one, *mon sergent.*"

"Nor through the office from the back there—from the cells?"

"No, *mon sergent*. There is nobody to come, all the cells are now empty, please, *mon sergent*, if you will forgive my mentioning it."

"Gaa-arh!" snarled the sergeant. "No one approached the desk at all? You are sure?"

"Certain, *mon sergent*. Why, have you then lost something?"

"No. Get on with your work."

When the clerk's head was once more bent over his ledgers, the sergeant opened the drawer into which he had put the money. He was agreeably surprised to find that it was still there and transferred it to his wallet. They were, after all, his bruises.

There happened to be a police patrol car in that area. Having received orders by radio, it swept up to the police-station door and its crew came hastily in, addressing the sergeant in tones of affectionate opprobrium and asking what the trouble was this time. "Lost a prisoner? Well, why didn't you lock him in?"

"I did," said the sergeant, almost in tears. "There are the keys, on that nail. They have never been off it. I glanced at them even as I started in pursuit. I am applying for a transfer."

"But—"

"I am applying for a transfer," said the sergeant firmly, and searched his desk for the appropriate application form. "There are too many peculiar things happening in this police station."

Charles and James Latimer ran up the stairs to Bibi le Vaseux's room and went in to find Mosset changing into an American suit. He had got as far as shirt and trousers and was cutting off the outlying parts of his beard with a pair of nail scissors preparatory to shaving. There was an American-pattern suitcase lying open on the bed; the lid and sides of it were decorated with colorful labels from, metaphorically speaking, China to Peru. Bibi was leaning over a small oil stove, encouraging a kettle to boil; Collet-serre was nowhere to be seen. James asked where he was.

"He's gone for a walk, gentlemen. He brought Monsieur Mosset here and then, as it seemed likely you'd be coming along, he went off quick-like," said Bibi.

"I thought I told you to go and get a taxi," said Charles sharply.

"He won't be ready for another 'alf hour yet," said Bibi with a jerk of his head towards Mosset.

Indeed, the photographer was in that condition of frantic haste which defeats its own purpose. The nail scissors were blunt, the beard was tough. Stray hairs entangled themselves in the hinge of the scissors and snatched them from his awkward fingers; when he caught them again he stabbed himself in the jaw with the points until tears of pain and exasperation rose in his eyes.

"This will never do," said Charles. "Sit down upon the bed and let me operate on you. Bibi, go and get that taxi at once, bid the man wait and come back here."

Bibi left the room and they could hear the stiff leg going down the stairs one tread at a time; bump-step, bump-step.

"Now he has gone," said Mosset, "I will tell you something. I must go back to my house."

"Impossible," said the cousins together.

"You will be rearrested at once," said James.

Mosset wrung his hands. "It is my packed bag. There is in it not only clothing but my other papers and nearly all my savings."

"Tell me where it is," said James. "I will go there at once and get it for you."

"But the police!" wailed Mosset. "They will be watching it in case I go back there."

"You are sure they have not found it already?" said Charles. "Keep your head still, pray!"

"No. They did not look in the right place."

"Where is the right place?" asked James.

"There is a kitchen behind my sitting-room," bleated Mosset. "Oh no, I cannot allow gentlemen like you to run my errands!"

"Sir," said James, "when gentlemen of my family embark upon any undertaking, be assured that they carry it through! Where is your bag?"

"There is a paraffin container—a drum with a tap—it stands in my kitchen upon an upturned wooden box. The bag is under the upturned box. But, sir—"

"I shall find it," said James.

"The train goes in half an hour," said Charles. "Meet us, Cousin, at the Gare de Lyon, if you will?"

James nodded and went out of the room; the door closed behind him.

"Now," said Charles, "can you shave yourself? Or had I better finish my task? Monsieur Mosset, sir, you look at the moment like a half-scraped coconut, if I may—"

"Has he gone?" asked Mosset.

"Who? My cousin? He is—halfway there by now."

"I did not hear him go down the stairs," said Mosset uneasily.

"Come," said Charles, lathering the shaving brush, "will you do this, or shall I? Quick, sir, the train will not wait."

Mosset took the shaving brush and set to work while Charles folded the discarded suit and packed it in the suitcase.

"You must remember that you are American. You know very little French, and that little badly pronounced. There will be no need to speak. When the taxi stops you call up a porter, give him your luggage and the seat reservation (here it is), and say 'Dijon, Dijon,' loudly. Here is also your travel ticket and some American dollar bills. Give the taxi driver two and the porter another. No one will stop an American who throws dollar bills about and cannot speak French. How is your poor face?"

"I have done," said Mosset, hastily washing up. "Sore but unremarkable. The collar—thank you. *Mon Dieu!* Is this a tie?"

"It is and you're going to wear it. Quickly!"

"I do not recognize myself," said Mosset, winding it round his neck, "I have no doubts now. How shall I ever repay—"

"Live happily ever after. Your jacket. The hat. Where the devil is Bibi?"

"Your excellent and noble cousin," began Mosset.

"Can perfectly well look after himself. Dark sunglasses with horn rims, put them on. Raincoat over your arm; I've got the suitcase—come!"

Bibi was pounding slowly up the stairs as they came down; he turned and led them through back doors and grimy yards into a court which had an archway upon a busy street where a taxi waited. Here Bibi stopped.

"Adieu," he said firmly.

Charles put Mosset into the taxi, shut the door, and told the driver to go to the Gare de Lyon, quick. The taxi swirled away and Charles turned upon Bibi, who backed.

"Adieu," he repeated.

"Provided," said Charles, "that you and that scoundrel Collet-serré never speak of us, never think of us, never even mention us between yourselves, this will indeed be *adieu* for ever. But if you are ever so stupid as to talk of what you have seen and heard, look behind your chair for I and my cousin will be standing there ready to "

"Stop, stop!" croaked Bibi. "We will forget, I have forgotten, to me you are as one already long dead."

Charles checked momentarily in the act of turning away and then broke into one of his peals of infectious laughter. He walked away with long strides, still laughing; Bibi leaned feebly against the side of the arch and watched him out of sight.

A flustered American arrived in a taxi at the Gare de Lyon. He had not much time before the train left and apparently he had neither French currency nor the French language.

He thrust his highly decorated suitcase at the porter and gave the taxi driver two dollar bills with frantic gestures to show it was the only money he had. The taxi driver did not mind in the least. The American turned on the porter, flapped his hands at him, and then seized him by the sleeve to drag him towards the train. The American's horn-rimmed tinted glasses did not fit very well, they slid down his nose, he pushed them up, they slid down—he waved his arms, crying "Dijon, Dijon!" in a loud voice. The porter asked him, with an explanatory gesture, if he had his ticket and the American plunged into a pocket for it and the seat reservation. The porter snatched them and ran with the worried little American trotting behind, holding his glasses with one firm finger against the bridge of his nose. They reached the train, which was standing at the platform; the porter found the right carriage, put the bag down upon the platform, and visibly expected his tip. He also received a dollar bill and poured out a flood of voluble French thanks which included some phrase about mugs with dollar bills. The American, who was in the act of carrying his own bag into the carriage, turned sharply and his glasses all but escaped him. He thrust them on again, went inside the train, and found his seat.

Two minutes later the Latimer cousins came unhurriedly along the platform; Mosset, who was looking for them, ran back to the door to meet them. James handed up Mosset's own bag, smelling almost audibly of paraffin.

"I was but just in time," he said. "The police came to the house, but I managed to avoid them."

Mosset began to try to thank them but was firmly checked. "You know how to deal with the American things, do you not?" said Charles. "You will find the name and address on a card inside the suitcase. I think, sir, that your train is about to start. I wish you Godspeed, Monsieur Mosset."

"I warmly concur," smiled James, and the train pulled out, leaving them on the platform.

Mosset pushed back his glasses for the fiftieth time and returned to his seat.

* * *

Two days later the Latimers strolled into their hotel in time to see the manager and the reception clerk gesturing excitedly over an American-pattern suitcase emblazoned with labels which had, it appeared, just been delivered to the hotel.

"It is the same," said the clerk. "I handled it myself and I recognize it."

"Also," said the manager, "it is addressed to him." He fingered the tie-on label attached to the handle. "Sent from Dijon. He is out at the moment, you say?"

"Gone to get a haircut, he should be back soon."

"We will keep it down here, then, till he comes."

James and Charles Latimer bought a couple of daily papers at the desk and retired to a seat not far from the suitcase to read them. Five minutes later its American owner came in, a pleasant man named Dexter. The Latimers knew him as a hotel acquaintance; his principal interest for them lay in the fact that in size and in the proportions of his build he was very like Mosset, the photographer.

Dexter waved cheerfully to the Latimers and came towards them, only to be intercepted by the reception clerk.

"Monsieur will excuse me—there is a suitcase here—"

Dexter looked, dived at it, and uttered a loud exclamation.

"I'll be damned! It's mine. Where did this come from?"

The clerk was understood to say that the carrier for the railways had delivered it, but Dexter was too excited to listen.

"Mr. Latimer—Major Latimer—see what's here! I was telling you two days ago this suitcase unaccountably vanished from my room here while I was out in the afternoon. Sure, sure, I told everybody. Well, now, look here, if this isn't the darnedest thing! Sent back from Dijon. Now, will somebody please tell a poor mutt how that came about?" He was patting the case and stroking the labels as though a lost pet had been restored to him. "It isn't so much the case, I could buy another, it's the labels. That one I regard as the gem of my collection. I was the first salesman of dentists' equipment to enter Yokohama after—"

"I understood you, sir, to say that you had also lost some items of clothing," said James, who naturally held mid-Victorian views about dentists. "Are they, by a happy chance, also returned?"

Dexter put the suitcase on the counter and threw the lid back. Inside, beautifully shrouded in tissue paper, was his missing suit, his hat, and his raincoat; his shirt and socks, washed and ironed, his tie, creaseless and glossy, and his shoes polished to a mirror finish. The American unfolded his suit with something like awe.

"It's been to the cleaner's! Just a minute, there was a small tear by this pocket I meant to— It's been mended. Can you beat it?"

"No, sir, I cannot," said Charles, who always became markedly more American when he was with Americans. "No, sir, I allow that that set of circumstances you have just disclosed is a world-beater, yes, sir."

"One point is made abundantly clear," said James. "Whoever the person may have been who stole your clothes—"

"Borrowed, sir, borrowed—"

"Borrowed your clothes, he is a gentleman."

But Dexter was digging under drifts of tissue paper like a St. Bernard rescuing a snowbound pilgrim.

"There is something else here," he said, and drew out two bottles of excellent burgundy of a vintage year.

By this time the manager had joined the party and he regarded the wine with something like reverence. "1929," he breathed. "Now, when that has been allowed a few days to settle—"

"Well," said Dexter, addressing the manager, "let me apologize for the all-fired fuss I kicked up the other day when I mislaid my case. I seem to remember saying things I would rather forget. This is my first visit to Paris, France, and if borrowing suitcases after this fashion is one of the customs of the country, write me down as one who likes it."

" 'And those who came to scoff,' " quoted James, " 'remained to pray.' "

CHAPTER XIV:
Traffic Jam

CHARLES AND JAMES LATIMER sat at a small table on the pavement outside a café in the Boulevard des Italiens, drinking coffee and watching the world go by. They sat there, not speaking much, and even Charles's natural vivacity seemed dimmed.

James broke suddenly into his short laugh, so like a barking dog, and Charles lifted heavy eyelids to ask him what was the joke.

"I was only thinking of what this street used to be like in our day. Tinkers, sitting on the pavement with all their tools spread round them, mending pots; a long-haired fellow who used to clip poodles—"

"I remember him very well. He needed clipping far more than did his clientele."

"And the lemonade sellers with gilded tanks on their backs."

"I remember best the day when four women came out staggering under a vast bundle. When they unrolled it, James, it was fluffy stuff out of a mattress. What did that fruit seller call it?"

"Flock, Charles, flock. I said that there was no doubt it must be wool, but she said it was not."

"When the women started to comb out the lumps, small pieces detached themselves and blew about like snowflakes, making everyone sneeze. You sneezed so violently that your hat flew off and a dog ran away with it."

James nodded solemnly. "I had to repair to a hatter's for a new one and there was only one in the shop which was large enough for me."

"But it was a very handsome beaver," said Charles, and yawned suddenly. "Cousin James, why were those days so much better than these?"

"Are they? I am by no means sure. Paris is cleaner—incredibly cleaner. The people are better clothed, better fed, there is more—"

"Yes, yes, I agree. I was not talking about the people, I meant ourselves. Look at us. We have enough money. If we run short we can—"

"Talking about money," began James, but Charles swept on unheeding.

"We are men in the prime of life and we shall not age. We have powers not only equal to other men's but vastly superior, and nothing can harm us or make us afraid since the worst thing which can happen to men happened to us eighty years ago. Why are we not happier?"

"I am," said James stoutly, and called up the waiter for some more coffee. "You know what is the matter with you, Charles? You have been using up energy too fast; we have not encountered our cousins for a week. We will go and spend an hour or two with them and receive quite literally a new lease of life. Cheer up. You are a little debilitated, but happily the remedy is simple."

"Battening like vampires," grumbled Charles. "I cannot like it, Cousin."

"Charles, it does not hurt them or we should not have been permitted to do it, you know that. They may feel a little unaccountably tired, but there is nothing that an extra hour's sleep will not restore. You know the conditions perfectly well. So long as we do good and not evil, it is allowed."

Charles changed the subject. "You said something about money, but I rudely interrupted you."

"It is the money we took at St. Denis-sur-Aisne. That shopkeeper fellow whom we robbed. We did rob him, Charles. Those suits and all the rest."

"Let us send him their value, then; we kept a note of what they cost. I suspect, Cousin James, that we shall then be paying him more promptly than he is used to being paid. Shopkeepers expect to wait, that is their lot in life," said the man who remembered 1870.

"I dare say that you are in the right, Cousin Charles. Let us send it, then, but how to do so safely?"

"There is a special kind of post for valuables," said Charles. "I was reading a notice about it the other day. It costs a little more, but safe delivery is assured."

James nodded. "There is also the money we took from the bank," he said. "You did maintain that France owed us that for our funerals, but—"

"Send it back," laughed Charles. "It is too late in the day to plague ourselves over a handful of old bones. The time for that is past and I know that memory irks you."

"We will pay that also," said James with a contented sigh. "I wish I could think of some means of telling our young cousins about the gold you and I put down the well at Oakwood Hall. I told that priest at the last moment that if any came to enquire after us they should be told to go and look where Truth reputedly dwells. He repeated it after me and said that he would note it down in writing, but I cannot tell whether he did so or not. Evidently no one of our family traced us to St. Denis-sur-Aisne."

Charles nodded agreement. "You did the best thing possible under agitating circumstances, Cousin James, in my opinion. Had the message been delivered, your sister Emma and various of the servants would remember where the well used to be before it was filled in. But now there is no one to remember, will anyone know that there was once a well in the north corner of your stable-yard?"

James's eyebrows went up in dismay. "I had not thought of that; you are in the right, Charles. My mind had not passed beyond ascertaining whether the message is still in existence and somehow bringing it to the notice of our young relatives."

"Difficult," murmured Charles, "very difficult."

"We cannot go from here to search for a lost message at St. Denis-sur-Aisne, it is too far from our cousins. We should be strengthless wraiths at that distance."

"Mere shimmers with vaguely human outlines."

"Would it be possible in some way to find out, in talk, whether they know of a filled-in well at home?"

"You will have to be extremely careful if you do try it," warned Charles. "Jeremy could, I believe, be hoodwinked, but our sweet Sally is wide awake indeed. I tell you, James, she half suspects us already."

"Of what?"

"Of not being what we seem."

"She may be percipient," said James. "Psychical, in the new jargon. You do not want to find yourself driven into a corner until you have to admit that you are her great-grandfather who died in 1870."

"She would either disbelieve it and us, in which case it would be of no use our telling her anything, or believe it, which might startle her so as to do her an injury. We cannot risk that."

"Certainly not," agreed Charles. "It is a dilemma. Here you are, practically holding a large sum of money of which Sally's family stand in need, and you cannot put them in possession of it because our story is one which it is virtually impossible to tell."

"They are in serious need of the money, are they not?" said James anxiously. "I myself had gathered that impression."

Charles nodded. "It appears that taxation is upon so oppressive a scale in England today that the older families are actually impoverished. Particularly is this true of what are called death duties. Sally told me that her father died last year and that her brother is having to sell some of the property to pay the tax upon the estate."

"What! Can one not even die without being heavily fined for so doing?"

"Apparently not. You and I, James, died in time. At least our families did not have to pay for the privilege of losing us."

"There are young sons to educate," said James. "Three, I think, and a girl or two, but of course the girls do not matter. A reliable governess will do for them, but it cost my father at least a hundred a year to send me to Eton. I gathered that our good Jeremy wanted to help in this matter, but the boys' father, Sally's brother, would not entertain the idea."

"Quite right," said Charles approvingly.

"Absolutely right. I told Jeremy so. But it weighs heavily upon my mind, Charles. We must think of some means of informing them about it."

"Of course," said Charles. "We must— Hello. Here they come in their splendid automobile. Shall we stop them?"

"By all means," agreed James.

The Rolls-Bentley came nosing through the traffic from the direction of the Opéra. The two elder Latimers did not even look at it; James was busy stirring up the last sugar in the bottom of his cup and drinking it, while Charles paid off the waiter. Nevertheless, when the big car was halfway across the Rue de Grammont-Taitbout intersection near which they were sitting, it stopped suddenly and utterly.

The Boulevard des Italiens is one of the main thoroughfares of Paris; it carries a heavy load of traffic night and day. It only needed, therefore, a car or two to attempt to cross the boulevard at the intersection, only to be foiled by the length of the Rolls-Bentley, for the traffic to begin to pack up on either side with horn-blowings and curses in several languages. The policeman on point duty ran from his post to tell Jeremy that it was *"absolument défendu d'arrêter là aucune automobile quelconque,"* which all sounded so indescribably menacing that poor Jeremy's French deserted him altogether.

"Je connais—I mean, *je sais. Je ne le—*Hell! I mean, the damn thing won't start."

"Allez," said the policeman, twirling his white traffic stick, *"allez, houp!"*

"Damn it, I'm not a circus," said Jeremy, scarlet in the face, and he leapt out from the driving seat to open the hood and put his head inside.

Charles's waiter looked past him with an amused expression and the American turned to see what the joke was. The waiter said that it was an auto which had planted itself there upon the crossroads and did not wish to proceed. Charles stared for a moment and then clapped James upon the shoulder.

"It is our cousins who are in trouble," he said, in French for the waiter's benefit.

"What? Where? God bless my soul. Let us go and try to help them."

They snatched up their hats and ran along the pavement to the corner, where they dived into the traffic, which had ceased to swirl and had become so clotted instead that it was difficult to pass between the cars. Charles edged past a long-nosed sports car to bow deeply, hat in hand, before Sally.

"Good day, Cousin Sally. I hope I see you in perfect health?"

"Oh yes, thank you, but very embarrassed. Isn't this dreadful, and the policeman is getting so cross with us!"

James sidled round the back of a baker's van and strode easily over the front wheel of a Vespa motorcycle to stand bareheaded at Sally's door. Charles made room for him by edging round to join Jeremy by the open bonnet. Jeremy was cursing steadily in the intervals of coherent speech.

"This is the second time she's done this. Can't be battery terminals again. When I get back to England—"

The traffic policeman put his head under the hood within three inches of Jeremy's and asked if Monsieur was going to remove his auto or must an Army Demolition Squad do what was necessary with dynamite? A lorry driver on the right offered some advice which it was to be hoped that Sally did not overhear, a baby Renault on the left offered a tow, and Jeremy tore his hair.

Charles leaned over his shoulder and twisted the distributor cap back and forth once or twice.

"Get in and start her," he said, closing the bonnet. "She will go now."

"But—" began Jeremy, but Charles overruled him.

"How do these fastenings work? Quick, before we stop all the traffic in Paris."

Jeremy, with a slightly glazed expression, snapped the hood locks, got into the driver's seat, and touched the starter. The engine sprang to life at once and the policeman said, "Ah!"

"Get in, get in, both of you," said Sally, as all the packed traffic be-

gan to move at once, "get in, or you'll be killed!" The elder Latimers
leapt into the back seat, one from either side, and hastily slammed the
doors before they could be swept off.

"Ma'am," said James, "your kind solicitude touches me deeply,
though the risk was not, perhaps, so great as it appeared."

Charles tapped him warningly on the ankle and Jeremy said that in
his opinion he himself had been in the greatest danger. "Another half
minute and that traffic cop would have brained me with that white club
of his. He was getting positively homicidal. But, Cousin Charles, how
did you work that little miracle?"

"Moral superiority, Cousin Jeremy, moral superiority. What, shall
immortal man be mastered by man-made machinery? Never."

"Well, I am," said Jeremy. "Not often, but this automobile can work
it. Maybe I'm not immortal enough, or something."

Sally looked over her shoulder to smile into Charles's laughing eyes.

"Darling, Cousin Charles Latimer is laughing at you."

"He has the right. Cousin Charles Latimer has rated himself a drink."
Jeremy swung the car round at the wide junction of the Boulevards des
Italiens and Haussmann and drove along to the Ambassador Hotel.
"There's one thing at least where I rate Paris above London; in Paris
you can drive to where you want to go, stop, get out, and leave the car
there. As here." He pulled the Rolls-Bentley in to the pavement; almost
before she stopped the elder Latimers were standing bareheaded at
Sally's door to hand her out. She led the way into the hotel with the two
cousins, hat in hand, half a pace behind on either side and Jeremy, with
his hands in his pockets and a thoughtful expression upon his face,
bringing up the rear with long slow strides. They went to the bar, where
Jeremy ordered drinks.

"And what about you, Cousin Charles?"

"The gentleman enjoyed a mint julep when he was here before,"
suggested the bartender.

"So I did, George, so I did," said Charles. "I would be glad to have
another. George, I will maintain in any company that your mint juleps
will not be beaten even in Old Virginia. No, sir."

"Thank you, sir. I was, in fact, shown how to make them by a Virginian gentleman."

When the various orders had been carried out, Jeremy said that
George looked better, did he not, than the last time the cousins were
there. "No more pink monkeys, George?"

"No, sir," said George.

"Did they ever catch that one?"

"I don't really believe, sir, thinking it over calmly, that there ever was one. I have come to the conclusion that there is more in telepathy than some people think. I was watching the Colonel pretty close that day, him being about due for one of his crisises, and I do believe he saw that monkey so plain he made me see it too. That's what I think."

"You are a very sensible level-headed fellow," said James approvingly, "by Jove, you are. Congratulate you."

"Not to deny that it gave me a turn at the time," admitted George.

"Never mind. What has become of our elderly friend, the Colonel?"

George smiled. "He has gone off drink altogether, sir. He has not been in this bar since that day."

Jeremy laughed aloud. "He stayed in bed for a couple of days after that little episode and since then he has taken up the pursuit of physical fitness in a big way. Oh brother, he has gotten himself a singlet and a pair of running shorts and he runs all around the blocks here at 7 A.M. on a cup of coffee and one biscuit."

"He has bought himself a pair of Indian clubs," bubbled Sally, "and only yesterday one of them got away from him and went through the window into the street and straight into a milk cart— Oh dear! Such a mess!"

"Did he break the window too?" asked James.

"Of course not," said Jeremy, "it was wide open."

Charles leaned apparently accidentally against James and murmured, "Another good deed," in his ear. James smiled covertly and George said that the old gentleman, meaning the Colonel, had taken on a new lease of life. "He looks twenty years younger, gentlemen, he does indeed."

Jeremy, reverting abruptly to a previous grievance, said that that was all very well but it did not explain what bug had bitten Rollo. He told the bartender in detail about how the Rolls-Bentley had stalled for no reason in the Boulevard des Italiens.

"It sounds," said George, "as though she was—" He hesitated for a word and added: *"Ensorcelée."*

"Come again?," said Jeremy.

"Bewitched, darling," explained Sally. "Under a spell. Don't you think Rollo must be bewitched, Cousin Charles?"

"It is an ingenious explanation, ma'am," said Charles calmly, "though if I were a motor mechanic I think I should look for other causes as well."

"But she went as soon as you touched her," said Jeremy. "That's what fazes me. You walk up and touch her and she goes. Why?"

"Coincidence, Cousin Jeremy, coincidence."

"Could be," said Jeremy doubtfully, "could be. But you were so sure she would go, and she did."

"Have it your own way, Cousin," said Charles, laughing. "If I can really walk up to stopped cars and say 'Go' and they go— Gentlemen, hush! They should use me instead of petrol."

Jeremy shook his baffled head in an attempt to clear it. "When you put it like that it does sound mad. Guess I was so rattled I didn't know what was happening."

"When I was a boy," said James, "and that seems a long time ago now, ignorant people in country districts still believed in witchcraft. If they thought there was a witch anywhere in their vicinity, they would obtain a branch of the tree called by some mountain ash and by others rowan and nail it above the door. No witch, so they believed, could pass by the mountain ash."

"There you are, darling," said Sally. "We'll get a bunch of rowan berries and tie them on Rollo's bonnet and have no more trouble."

"It was equally as efficacious," said James, "to grow a specimen of *Pyrus aucuparia* in the garden, preferably close beside the door or doors of the house."

"If you suppose," said the baited Jeremy, "that I'm turning Rollo into a perambulating shrubbery to keep off witches when all I've probably got is an air lock somewhere in the fuel-supply line, you've got another think coming to you." He stopped and thought over what he had just said. "Sorry, folks. Guess that sounded peevish, I didn't mean it that way. It's only these unexplained stops are a bit worrying."

Charles dropped a friendly hand on his shoulder. "My dear fellow, we all think you took it very well. I don't suppose it will happen again."

"I certainly hope not. Sally and I thought of taking a little run out tomorrow around the River Loire to cast an eye over some of these much-advertised chateaux. Stay a night somewhere, maybe. What about you two coming along with us? Delighted to have you come and maybe Rollo'll behave with you aboard."

"Do come, Cousin James and Cousin Charles," said Sally. "Such fun, and you can keep the bogies off us, can't you?"

CHAPTER XV:
The Ghost-Hunters

THEY WALKED UP many winding steps to admire wonderful carving and splendid stained-glass at Chartres. James bought a handbook; they had lunch and proceeded to Tours, where they looked at churches and James bought a handbook. They turned upriver at Tours and came to Amboise where, in 1560, the principal industry was the massacre of Huguenots.

James bought a handbook, but when Sally had skimmed through its pages they all returned to the car and departed for Blois.

"Look," said Jeremy, "we came here to see châteaux. Right? Wrong? Cross out the one that doesn't fit. So far we've seen churches where famous people are buried and castles where they practiced murder as a fine art." He yawned suddenly "Let Cousin James buy a few more handbooks as we pass and then we'll find a nice quiet hotel someplace. We'll all have dinner and take the handbooks up to read in bed." He yawned again. "Excuse me."

"There is an uncommon fine château just ahead," said James. "The Château de Chaumont. Catherine de' Medici lived there."

"What was she famous for?" asked Jeremy.

"Poisoning, chiefly," said Charles cheerfully.

"Pass, Catherine de' Medici, and all's well," said Jeremy. "How much farther to Blois?"

"Just over ten miles," said Sally after a short pause for mental arithmetic.

"Just ahead of us," said James, "about three miles beyond the Château de Chaumont, is a little place called Vermanie. It is a small town with very old houses in it and a ruined castle—"

"Cousin," interrupted Jeremy, "I'm nearly a ruin myself, I don't want to look at any more."

"I was about to say," continued James, "that Vermanie contains a small but excellent inn, the Golden Cockerel. There are not many bedrooms, twenty, possibly; the place is run by a man and his wife. She cooks, and ah! her omelettes. For a main dish, there is a *specialité de la maison* of pullets cooked in wine and seasoned with mushrooms which is vivid in my memory. Her soup—"

"That'll do," said Jeremy. "I begin to revive already. We will stop at the Golden Cockerel."

"Do you also know this place, Cousin Charles?" asked Sally.

"Why, no, ma'am. I have never been in these parts before. James's knowledge of France is much more extensive than mine."

"The inn itself is very old; it dates from the fifteenth century," said James.

"But not, I hope, the beds," said Sally.

"Or the plumbing," said Jeremy. "Never mind. I am prepared, Cousin, to overlook a few gurgles and pops in the hand-basins for such cooking as you describe."

"Much of the medieval furniture is still *in situ*," pursued James. "I remember, for example, a magnificent carved oak dresser in the hall and a very early sixteenth-century settle in the alcove beside the fire.

The people who keep it are named Ducros, Hippolite Ducros and his wife Angelique. He had a really splendid black beard."

They drove on in silence until a turn of the road brought them within sight of Vermanie upon its hill. There was the gapped and broken wreck of a castle upon the hilltop; the little town straggled down the slope to touch, with a jetty like a stumpy finger, the shining links of Loire. The road to Blois crossed the town at the Place des Medici; Jeremy, under James's guidance, turned right to find the hotel of the Golden Cockerel facing him at the top of the square. The house was plainly very ancient, its stone walls and little round turrets blackened with age, but fresh white curtains hung at windows bright with cleanliness and a brass knocker and doorhandle glittered in the rays of the setting run. They drew up at the front door and the landlord came out to greet them, a small fair man, clean-shaven and wearing a black apron. He came forward, smiling, and Jeremy asked if he were the landlord.

"I am, monsieur, to serve you."

"Could we have dinner, do you think?"

"But certainly, monsieur. Be pleased to enter."

They went in, Sally escorted as usual by the elder Latimers. The hall was a large, low-ceilinged room with a great open fireplace beside which there was an alcove containing a high-backed settle of walnut, dark with age. Opposite the fireplace there was what James had described as a dresser; the cupboard doors were heavily carved with armorial bearings and the shelves bore jugs and plates of the cheerful pottery made at Quimper in Brittany. For the rest, the place had been furnished as a lounge with comfortable chairs and small tables and was further embellished by a most entrancing smell of cooking. There was a small bar at the far end and a flight of stairs leading upwards.

"Dinner in ten minutes?" said the landlord. "Madame would perhaps wish to wash her hands. I will call my wife." He went out by a door near the stairs and Sally turned to smile at James.

"You were quite right, Cousin James. This place is charming."

"I am delighted, ma'am, that it meets with your approval."

"There's only one thing missing," said Jeremy, "and that's the gentleman with the black beard."

"No doubt," said Charles rather hastily, "the place has changed hands."

"It couldn't matter less," said Jeremy. "What about stopping over a night here, Sally?"

"I'll see the bedrooms when I go upstairs. I should think it would be all right here."

A very large and very stout woman came into the hall and greeted them pleasantly. *"Bonsoir, madame. Bonsoir, messieurs.* Would Madame care to come upstairs? A little care is needed, these stairs are so old that they are uneven. Yes, but perfectly safe, oh, perfectly, madame. Of a most unexampled solidity. Shall I lead the way, if Madame permits?"

The dinner was all that James had promised and they returned, soothed and comforted, to the lounge to find a fire in the huge grate, since the September evenings grew chilly. Jeremy sank into an armchair with a deep sigh of content.

"They certainly know how to look after you here. If our cousins will excuse me, I won't stay up long. I don't know why it is that driving these days makes me so sleepy, it never used to. I've driven in America for eight hours practically on end and not been like this. Must be the air or something." He yawned. "Don't let me drag you up earlier than you want, Sally. Guess I'll just get my head down and let nature do the rest."

"I'll come up with you," said Sally. "There are some other people staying here and I suppose they'll be coming in soon. I don't feel I want to talk to a lot of strangers tonight."

"Oh, are there indeed?" said James. "Do you know who they may be?"

"Some kind of society," said Sally. "Antiquarians of some sort, I think. Madame said they were interested in old houses."

"They do not sound the sort of persons to disturb your slumbers," said Charles.

"I can't figure any antiquarian society rip-snorting around to keep folks awake," said Jeremy. "Quiet and peaceful here, isn't it? Cousin James, you picked a winner here and I hand it to you. What a dinner. Guess I've eaten too much." He heaved himself out of his chair. "Well, I'm going up while my legs will still carry me."

They said good night and trailed off, tired but happy, and the cousins settled down by the fire. The landlord came in, served them with wine from the bar, and accepted a glass himself.

"I gather that we are not your only guests tonight," said James.

The landlord said that he had, in fact, a party of about a dozen people staying for a few days. "They arrived from England only today, ten gentlemen and two ladies."

"A nice proportion," murmured Charles. "The ladies should enjoy themselves."

"They are, perhaps, the wives of two of the gentlemen," suggested James.

"No, monsieur, they are single ladies, two friends."

"Antiquaries, are they not?" went on James, who was merely talking out of politeness.

"Pardon, monsieur?"

"Archaeologists. Students of ancient monuments."

"Oh no, monsieur. They are ghost-hunters."

"What!" said Charles, sitting up suddenly. "Did you say ghost-hunters?"

The landlord laughed. "To me, also, it appears absurd. Like Monsieur, I do not believe in ghosts, but there are many who do, very many. I ought to believe in them, they serve me very well here."

"How can that be?"

"The castle above on the hill is said to be a gathering place for ghosts, particularly the dungeons. It may be, they are gloomy enough. There is also an empty house, it is of great age, it dates back to our Francis the First. It is deserted because, they say, it is so infested with ghosts one cannot live in it. These places are well known, gentlemen, and parties of ghost-hunters come here to visit them from many lands, not only England but also Germany, Belgium, and Italy, and even Spain. They all come to the Golden Cockerel, that is why I said that the ghosts had served me well."

"It is fantastic," said James. "How say you, Charles?"

"I say that if I were a ghost I might resent being hunted," said Charles, laughing. "Tell me, landlord, does their prey never retaliate?"

"I never heard that they do——"

"No sly pinches? No tripping up in dark passages? No pins inserted in tender spots?"

"I believe not, monsieur——"

"What wasted opportunities!"

"When in the course of nature," said the landlord, "Monsieur becomes a ghost himself—may he live many happy years—he could perhaps arrange to have things reorganized upon a better plan."

"You must remember that, Charles," said James.

"But, indeed, it would seem that the ghosts, if they exist, do resent these intrusions," said the landlord, becoming serious. "For more than two years now these ghost-hunters have told me that they have had no results from their researches. They are beginning to say that it is no longer worth their while to come here. My business will suffer."

"You think that the ghosts are tired of being hunted and have gone away," said Charles. "One could not blame them, could one?"

"In fairness, no," admitted the landlord, "but it still remains bad for business."

"Is there," asked James, "no means known of attracting these—er—phenomena?"

"I have heard that ghosts are apt to haunt the scene of a murder," said the landlord.

"The solution is obvious," said Charles. "You must murder somebody."

"Is Monsieur suggesting that we should poison one of our guests?"

"Not while we are staying here," said James firmly.

"Besides," added Charles, "I assume that such a course would only result in this house becoming infested. I gather you would not desire that."

"It would not do at all," said the landlord. "My wife would never permit it. To speak more seriously, nothing supernatural has ever been seen or heard in this house, though there is a story that a guest in my grandfather's time saw crocodiles sliding across this hall. But no one else has ever seen them."

"They may have been spirituous rather than spiritual," suggested James.

"I agree with Monsieur. Excuse me, I think I hear my party returning."

He went to the front door and opened it while Charles leaned across to James and spoke in a low tone.

"He is a nice fellow and keeps an excellent table. It would be a thousand pities if he could not continue here."

James nodded. "This ghost-hunting, how is it done?"

"We will find out."

The party trooped in, blinking in the light after the darkness outside, for it was after eleven o'clock. There were two ladies a little past their first youth, a little skinny and over-eager. They were followed by a group of men who, as is usual when more than four people enter a room at once, were merely a bunch of forms recognizably human, just as a herd of twenty cows to a townsman is one cow twenty times repeated. There were, actually, only ten men, but there seemed many more as they weaved about the room unburdening themselves of boxes and coils of wire which they piled upon the dresser or dropped into corners.

James and Charles rose to their feet as the ladies entered and stood back, side by side, in the alcove by the settle. The ladies acknowledged the courtesy with awkward half-smiles and little cries of "Please don't get up" and "Don't let us disturb you." The Latimers bowed politely and remained standing; the ladies made a dart at the fireplace, rubbing their hands and exclaiming that they were chilly, and the room filled with voices. The landlord asked if the party had had a successful evening and a tall thin man with a lined face and strong glasses said, "No. Not a sausage," which, being translated literally into French, cast the landlord into confusion.

"You desire sausages? Certainly, if you wish, I will tell my wife."

"No, no. Not to eat. Merely a way of saying that we have seen nothing."

"You are returned early," said the landlord. "It is not yet midnight."

"It was cold," said the tall man, "the ladies were tired, and then it came on to rain. There is always tomorrow."

"Very true," said the landlord. "The sandwiches you ordered are ready for you in the dining room."

The tall man, who appeared to be in some sense the leader of the band, raised his voice.

"Come along, ladies an' gents. Supper in the dining-room."

They all trooped after him except one big heavy-shouldered man with a mustache and a monocle and the unmistakable stamp of the British Army. He had remained standing just inside the front door until the room cleared, when he came slowly forward, leaned on the back of one of the armchairs, and looked at the Latimers.

"Good evening, gentlemen," he said pleasantly. "You staying here too?"

"Merely lodging for the night," said James, "we shall proceed upon our way in the morning."

"Not ghost-hunters?"

"Why, no, sir," said Charles. "We do not feel any need to look for them."

"Quite right. I joined this society to see some fun. No fun at all. Not even ghosts. Frightfully serious these people are, you'd never credit it. Notice the tall feller with the specs? He's the secretary. Organizer. Mustn't make jokes about ghosts to him. Oh lord, no, not the done thing at all. I want a drink." He paused, drew a long breath, and bellowed, "Landlord!" in a voice which rattled the glasses on the bar. The landlord appeared instantly.

"You called, monsieur?"

"I want a drink," said the big man in rugged British French. "Have you any whiskey?"

"I have a little, monsieur."

"Excuse me," said Charles, "but whiskey is not very good in France and excessively dear. If you can bear to drink brandy —"

"Try me," said the big man. "What are you gentlemen having?"

The Latimers thanked him and said that a little cognac would perhaps go down well; the newcomer amended his order and they all gathered round the bar.

"May as well introduce myself. Orleby-Appleton, Major. Well, here's luck."

"Sir, your very good health," said James. "Our name is Latimer."

"Brothers?"

"No, cousins. My cousin is Major Latimer of the American Army of the South."

"From the South, eh?" said Orleby-Appleton, mishearing the preposition. "From Texas, by any chance?"

"No, sir," said Charles. "I am a Virginian."

"Indeed. Knew a feller from Texas at one time. Very decent feller. Name of Smith. You might have known him." The Major looked at his empty glass; Charles took the hint and ordered another round.

"May I ask, Major," said James, "whether you have long been a member of this society?"

"About six months."

"And how do you set about hunting ghosts?"

"My dear chap, how do I know? They all run about with patent thermometers and bags of flour and balls of string. I don't butt in. There aren't enough balls of string and flour bags to go all round the party as it is. I just sit back and wait for 'em to produce their ghosts."

"And do they?"

"Not that I've noticed. There were some bumping noises in a house near Guildford we went to and they all got very excited. Myself, I think it was rats. Or a cat. Or both."

Charles broke into a laugh. "You do not appear to me, sir, to be a very enthusiastic believer. One almost wonders, if you will not regard it as an impertinence, why you joined."

"Your glass is empty," put in James. "Allow me. Landlord!"

"Thank you, thank you," said Orleby-Appleton. "A very fine cognac. No, gentlemen, if you were a poor devil of an ex-Army officer with no family, living in a couple of rooms on the damned miserable pittance Britain thinks adequate for a retirement pension, you'd look round for something amusin' to do in the evenings that wouldn't cost too much. That's why."

"And an excellent reason, too," said James warmly. "Britain has always been niggardly with her Service pensions. The scandal is notorious."

Charles, seeing that it was coming round again to Orleby-Appleton's turn to buy the round of drinks, excused himself and went away to buttonhole the secretary when the party had finished supper.

The ghost-hunters drifted out of the dining-room in twos and threes and hung about undecidedly as people do who cannot make up their minds to go to bed. Charles found it a simple matter to enter into conversation with them, and they were only too eager to tell him all about their methods. The flour sprinkled upon floors to reveal the trace of footsteps and the strings tied across passages or doorways to defeat any chance of fraud. "For we take our researches very seriously, Mr. Latimer," said the secretary. "We are not to be hoodwinked by practical jokers."

"No, no," said Charles earnestly.

"It is just as important—by the way, my name is Pullinger—to avoid false conclusions as to obtain true ones."

"I am convinced that you are in the right," said Charles.

"Ghosts," said Pullinger passionately, "are not a joke."

"No, indeed."

"Although," added Pullinger with a self-conscious laugh, "we do allow ourselves just a pleasant touch of frivolity in the name of our society." He took a card from his wallet and handed it to Charles; it read:

THE GLENTHORNE GHOST-HUNTERS DISCORPORATE.
GLENTHORNE. HAMPSHIRE.
HON. SEC: TIMOTHY PULLINGER.
WOOD END. GLENTHORNE. HANTS.

" 'Discorporate' I consider a pleasant touch. It has a double meaning: we are not an incorporated society and the ghosts are discorporate."

Charles just stopped himself from saying, "Gentlemen, hush!" and merely hazarded a guess that Pullinger had thought of that word himself.

"Well, you force me to admit the soft impeachment. I did, but we won't talk about that."

"These thermometers," prompted Charles.

"One infallible sign of an impending manifestation," said Pullinger, his Adam's apple wobbling on his thin neck, "is a sudden and-otherwise unaccountable fall in temperature. It may fall as much as ten degrees Fahrenheit or even more, though as a rule not so much as ten degrees Fahrenheit. We have, as part of our equipment, special thermometers fitted with a dial upon which a hand revolves after the manner of a one-handed clock. They are made in the U.S.A. We have one of them here—let me show you. Where is it? Where is the thermometer? Johnson, where is the thermometer? Wilson, Ashly, where is the thermometer? Miss Griggs, Miss Paulson, have you seen the—"

"Here is it," said one of the men, "on the floor in the corner."

"Please pick it up and put it somewhere safe. It will be trodden on or kicked if it is left on the floor. Please put it on that chair in the corner; one cannot be too careful with expensive equipment, can one? Dear me, no. Well, now, Mr. Ridley—"

"Excuse me," said Charles. "Latimer."

"Latimer, of course, Latimer. Now, what association of ideas made me call you Ridley? Of course! Of course! These two poor suffering wretches at the stake at Oxford. 'We shall this day light such a candle, Master Ridley,' eh? We learned all about it at school, did we not? How these little things stick, do they not?"

"I guess, sir," said Charles, "that the unfortunate gentlemen concerned did not think it such a little thing."

"Well, no. Of course not. Well, here is our thermometer, Mr. Latimer. You see that though it is a normal thermometer inside, the large dial upon the outside connected with it is so arranged as to magnify the effect of any rise or fall in temperature in such a way as to be readily observable even in poor light, such as we usually work by. Ingenious, is it not?"

"It is indeed," said Charles, who had had nearly enough of Mr. Pullinger. "Well, sir, now I notice that nearly everyone seems to be partaking of a small drink of some kind, will you have one with me?"

"Thank you, Mr. Latimer, that is very kind of you, but I never touch alcohol. Never have and never will. If they keep some simple form of fruit juice at the bar, I should be most happy to accept."

"I will find out what they stock," said Charles, and weaved his way through the crowd towards the bar.

CHAPTER XVI:
Cold Hands

CHARLES SLIPPED quietly out of the hall by the door leading to the kitchen. There had been a reference to "our refrigerator" during dinner and the Latimer cousins had become conversant with refrigerators and their uses. Most refrigerators contained ice cubes. He found himself in a short passage leading to the kitchen; probably the refrigerator would be there somewhere. It was; so was the landlord's wife, but she could not see him, nor was it now necessary for him to open the refrigerator door in order to get at what was inside it.

He gathered up a double handful of ice cubes and returned to the hall with them. When he had disposed of them to advantage he returned to the kitchen passage for a moment and then re-entered the hall. Miss Griggs saw him come out and fluttered up to him.

"Oh! Do tell me, Mr.—er—er—"

"Latimer," said Charles, bowing. "Major Latimer, ma'am, of the American Army."

"Oh, indeed! How interesting! Pleased to meet you, as I understand you say in America."

"Thank you, ma'am, I am indeed privileged to know you."

Miss Paulson swam up, glass in hand; she was too large for Miss Griggs to pretend she did not notice her.

"Oh! Clarissa, dear, this is Major Latimer of the American Army. Miss Paulson."

"Miss Paulson," repeated Charles, bowing again, "and Miss Griggs, I am indeed fortunate in meeting two such charming ladies in one evening. It must be my lucky night."

Miss Paulson giggled. "Really, Major Latimer! The things you Yankees say!"

Charles was so indignant that he actually snorted.

"Miss Paulson, ma'am, I have the honor to be a Southerner. Miss Griggs, ma'am, I believe you were about to ask me something?"

"Oh yes. Do tell me, where does that door go to?"

Charles looked at the service door through which he had just come. "Why, ma'am, I guess it just remains right on its hinges."

"Yes, yes. I meant, of course, where does it lead to?"

"Only to the kitchen, ma'am."

Miss Paulson said, "Really, Amabel!" in a tone well above a whisper and Charles disliked her more than ever. Poor Miss Griggs blushed hotly and drew back; Charles begged to be excused. "My cousin desires to speak to me."

He returned to the bar, ordered a small tumbler of orange squash, and made his way across the room towards Pullinger, who was addressing a group upon the importance of keeping tabulated records. Charles noticed in passing that Miss Griggs and Miss Paulson, together in a corner, appeared to be having what are rightly called Words. "I'll give you Yankees," murmured Charles. "You wait. Horrible woman."

He came to anchor beside Pullinger, offered the orange squash, and apologized for having been so long. Pullinger said please, not to apologize, and introduced the other men, one of whom said that it was a pity, wasn't it, that they had had a disappointing evening. Pullinger said that they would try again tomorrow night at the Old Mayor's House.

"Not here?" said Charles. "Is it of no use attempting to get results here? Surely, gentlemen, this house is old enough."

"Age is not all," said Pullinger. "Other factors are needed for conditions favorable to manifestations. We are not yet clear what these are, but—"

"Correct me if I am wrong," said Charles. "I understood you to say that a sudden drop in temperature was an indication? Your thermometer—"

He pointed to it where it sat on a chair self-consciously displaying a temperature of forty-two degrees Fahrenheit. Even as they stared, the needle stirred and went back another degree, not remarkable, considering the ice cubes which had been packed round the bulb.

Pullinger uttered a loud exclamation and issued a series of orders which were promptly carried out by the more experienced members present. All the lights were switched out except a small one over the bar, and this was hastily shaded by having a blue handkerchief draped over it. There was, of course, the firelight; since it was a wood fire in good working order, the leaping flames threw a romantic light about the room. The ladies retreated to the stairs and leaned over the handrail; the men of the party effaced themselves against the walls and all waited, scarcely breathing, to see what should come. Major Orleby-Appleton remained by the bar with an expression of sardonic amusement.

Charles leaned across the bar and asked in a whisper for a small glass of port; the landlord, fumbling in the dim light, managed to serve him. Charles drew it towards him but did not drink it, he merely tapped the bar softly and absent-mindedly and looked about the room. Then he leaned across to James and whispered in his ear.

"Come back in the corner here, Cousin, a moment. Listen. Now let us give these ghost-hunters something to remember."

James nodded eagerly. "It will be a kind deed," he murmured, "it will please them and profit the landlord."

"Will you act the ghost, Cousin? You ought to know how they are supposed to behave from those ghost stories you are continually reading."

"But they will recognize me," objected James. "I cannot make myself look like anyone else, you know that. The Basic Principle of Ultimate Truth imposed upon our Order absolutely forbids it. Whoever heard of a ghost who looked like someone else?"

"Very true," whispered Charles, "but there is no Basic Principle against putting a sheet over your head. Take one off your bed."

"And what will you do, Charles?"

"I will improve the occasion in divers ways. Leave it to me. Off with you, it is—it is the appointed hour!"

Back in the dark shadow under the stairs nobody noticed that James was no longer there. The silence became eerie, and when the fire slipped and fell together everyone jumped.

The hush was broken by Orleby-Appleton. "Is this part of your show, Pullinger? Or is the little beast real?"

There was a small monkey standing upright on the bar. He was dressed in a jacket and cap and could be seen quite plainly in the blue glimmer from the bar light. He had in one paw a glass of port from which he was slowly drinking, in the other paw he held the end of his own tail, a pose uncannily reminiscent of an Edwardian lady holding up the skirt of her long dress. Pullinger came across the room with quiet strides and the monkey bowed politely. Pullinger obviously did not believe in ghostly monkeys who drank port; he came steadily on and made a snatch at the animal. Even as his fingers closed upon it there was nothing there except the empty wineglass which was left in his hands.

The landlord leaned heavily upon the bar and addressed Secretary Pullinger in tones suitably low but nonetheless incisive.

"Monsieur. It is with delight that I entertain your group and provide food, drink, and accommodation. But it must be clearly understood that you entertain your ghosts elsewhere. What? If you were a football team you would not expect to kick your ball about in my house? I cannot permit that you play your ghost games here."

"It is no game," said Pullinger between his teeth. He was trying to set down the wineglass, which persisted in sticking to his fingers. This was only natural since Ulysses had spilt the wine down the stem. What was less natural was that when Pullinger had succeeded in setting it down and was turning away it was gently replaced in his hand.

Major Orleby-Appleton, still the complete skeptic, intervened.

"I don't know how you worked that monkey business, Pullinger, but that wineglass trick is simple. Elastic, sir, black elastic."

"Not with my glasses, monsieur, please," said the landlord. He took the wineglass firmly from Pullinger's fingers, washed and dried it, and put it back on the shelf. To Pullinger's faint surprise, it stayed there.

There came a deep groan from the far end of the hall near the chair upon which the thermometer was standing; all eyes turned towards it as an amorphous white patch appeared and grew to the size of a man entirely sheeted in white. It grew out of the wall, moaning wearily, then detached itself and drifted uncertainly about the room. The enthralled observers saw clearly that the chairs and tables standing about presented no obstacle to the figure, it merely passed unhurriedly through them without disturbing even the cigarette ash in the ashtrays. Finally, with a low bubbling wail, it wavered across to the fire and disappeared into it.

There was a prolonged sigh as the ghost-hunters, who had all been holding their breath, let it out together. The silence fell again, only to be broken by a short fat man with a bald head which gleamed in the firelight.

"I say, Pullinger."

"Yes, Mr. Gateshead?"

"Should you not have spoken to that poor unquiet spirit?"

"I did not consider it advisable, Mr. Gateshead. Without wishing to alarm the ladies, the aura surrounding that apparition was definitely evil."

"I don't agree with—" began Gateshead, and stopped abruptly as the log basket beside the fire rose, ejected its contents, and sailed through the air to come to rest upside down over Pullinger's head. Since the basket was large and deep, it extinguished him to the elbows and he had something of a struggle to be rid of it. A wild peal of falsetto laughter ran rapidly round the room just below the ceiling and ended with a deep gurgle in the electric-light fitting in the centre.

"Oh, my goodness!" exclaimed Gateshead.

"That," said Pullinger, mopping a scratch on his ear, "was a poltergeist."

"Seemed to me," said a little man wearing incredibly strong glasses, "as though it didn't like what you said about the other one, Pullinger."

"Landlord," said Orleby-Appleton, "I want a drink. Give me a nice glass of lemonade."

"Lemonade, monsieur. But certainly."

"On second thoughts, landlord, put a snifter of gin into it."

"Certainly, monsieur."

Orleby-Appleton peered into the dark corner at the end of the bar under the stairs.

"Landlord, ask those two gentlemen— Where are they?"

"Not there now, sir."

"Didn't see them go," grumbled the Englishman.

"Nor I, monsieur, but they have been gone some time."

The quiet air was suddenly rent by an earsplitting scream from Miss Paulson upon the stairs, followed by shrieks of "Cold hands! Cold hands! Aa-ah!" She twisted away from the handrail, missed her footing, and rolled slowly down to the bottom. Pullinger rushed to help her, but the bag of flour, which had been set upon the dresser, was hurled violently across the room. It hit the newel post of the stair just above the stooping Pullinger and burst, covering him and the lady with flour and filling the air with the fine powder. The white sheeted form, which had previously vanished into the fire, rose slowly out of the middle of the floor and continued to rise until it disappeared through the ceiling. At this point a sort of bluish wildfire flickered madly about the room and by its light the figure of the monkey could be seen, dancing excitedly upon the mantelpiece. What was, perhaps, even more shocking was that Pullinger was dancing too, a sort of Egyptian dance of stamping heavily back and forth with convulsive jerks of the body and slappings of himself with both hands, now in front and now behind, and all the time he did not speak nor cry out.

Suddenly, from just outside the window, a cock crowed loudly. Instantly the wildfire went out, the monkey vanished, and only Pullinger's uneven steps could be heard. Somebody switched on the lights upon a scene of disorder and a fire almost extinct; only Pullinger's unseemly posturings continued.

"Pullinger!" roared Gateshead. "Heavens, man, have you gone mad?"

"It is the *danse du ventre*," said Orleby-Appleton calmly. "Seen it in Cairo. Girls."

Pullinger stopped suddenly, unfastened the belt which alone held up his trousers, and shook himself. Something long, dark, and thin slid out of his trouser leg and wriggled rapidly away under a chair.

"Ah," said Pullinger contentedly, "that's better." He refastened his belt.

"It's an eel," said a man who had tipped back the chair to look. "It's a real eel. Someone put it down your neck, Pullinger.".

"Doubtless it comes out of my tank," said the landlord coldly. He advanced slowly upon the eel, made a sudden pounce, and captured it. "I prefer not to know," he added with some dignity, "which of you gentlemen saw fit to take an eel out of my eel-tank and bring it into the hall." He walked towards the service door with the eel writhing and flapping round his arms.

"It was the poltergeist," said Pullinger, and the landlord turned in the doorway.

"Bah!" he said, and walked out.

The Latimer cousins were standing together by the bar. Miss Paulson was sitting on the bottom stair, having reasonably quiet hysterics, and most of the others were white-faced and shaking. Only Miss Griggs, leaning over the balustrade like Juliet from her balcony, had pink cheeks and shining eyes and her hands were full of flowers. A keen observer might have noticed that the flower stalks were wet; this was not surprising, since they had been hastily snatched from the dining-room vases.

The company stared round upon each other, relieved to find that they were all there and not even hurt. Major Orleby-Appleton warmly congratulated the secretary.

"Good show, Pullinger. Excellent show. Can't think how you did it."

Pullinger cast a withering glance at him, but the Major did not see it. He finished his fortified lemonade, said good night to the company, and walked off upstairs to bed.

The landlord returned without his eel and Pullinger smiled appealingly upon him.

"Now, landlord. I'm afraid we've made your nice room in rather a mess. If you'll kindly lend us a couple of brooms, a dustpan and brush and a few dusters, we'll soon put things to rights."

"I thank Monsieur," said the landlord with great firmness, "but I should greatly prefer it to be left to my cleaners who come in early in the morning. They will deal with it, monsieur. Again, thank you." He gestured politely towards the stairs and even Pullinger thought it better not to argue. The party trailed off up the stairs, taking with them the convalescent Miss Paulson. Miss Griggs had already disappeared, taking her flowers with her. The Latimer cousins went last of all and paused to speak to the landlord.

"I fear your ghost-hunters have left you a deal of cleaning to do," said James, looking distastefully round the room.

"I am sorry that you should be so discommoded," said Charles, turning his brilliant smile on the landlord.

"Not at all, monsieur, not at all," said the landlord cheerfully. "A little something can be added to their bill and I need not pay my cleaners anything extra. It all helps, monsieur."

"So it does," said Charles, "so it does."

He and James went upstairs together and along the passage; when James reached the door of his bedroom, instead of opening it he walked straight into it with a loud bump and recoiled, rubbing his nose.

"I forgod," he said thickly. "Lasd dime I game ub I was nod maderialized." He applied a large white handkerchief just as the next door opened and Pullinger's head came out.

"I heard a typical hollow thud," he said eagerly.

"Another manifestation—"

"Dear me, no," said James, blowing his nose. "I carelessly and inadvertently struck against the door. Pray let me apologize for any disturbance."

"You might say," added Charles, "that the bump occurred because my cousin forgot that he was not a ghost."

Pullinger sniggered appreciatively and withdrew.

Charles helped James to remake his bed, disordered by having had a sheet ripped off in haste. "We were thoughtless," said Charles. "We should have taken the sheet from Pullinger's bed."

"I did not then know which is his room," said James. "It would never do to have inconvenienced the ladies. By the way, Charles, what did you do so to delight the lady on the stairs?"

"I only kissed her hand and put the flowers in it. The other woman had put her out of countenance."

"And the eel?"

"They live in a glass tank in the kitchen."

"To be fresh if one should order eel, no doubt," said James.

"No doubt. Cousin James, never again will I mock at you for reading ghost stories. Your performance was masterly, it nearly frightened me."

"When I was mortal," said James, "I used to take delight in reading of travels and adventures such as I could never come by in my own person. Now I read ghost stories. It is the same thing."

"Dear James," said Charles, "there is no one like you. Good night, and pleasant dreams."

In the morning, when the Latimers were all packed and ready to start, Sally noticed for the first time a small dark oil painting hanging on the wall near the top of the stairs. It showed the head and shoulders of a man in late middle life and he had a luxuriant black beard. She stopped to look at it, and Madame, wife of the proprietor, came up the stairs at that moment.

"Madame is looking at the portrait of my husband's grandfather," she said. "Hippolite Ducros."

"Indeed," said Sally. "Did he also own this hotel?"

"But certainly, madame. He and his wife, Angelique, made it the place it is. They were famous in their day."

Sally remembered James Latimer speaking of Hippolite and Angelique Ducros. Of course names are handed down in families.

"Your husband," she said, "is he also Hippolite Ducros?"

The woman laughed. "Not even Ducros, madame. The old Hippolite there, he had only one daughter, my husband's mother. Our name is Gaudet."

"Indeed," said Sally faintly, "how very interesting."

She went slowly down the stairs. Hippolite Ducros had a black beard. Sally stopped suddenly.

"Madame Gaudet! Excuse me—forgive my asking. What is your Christian name?"

"Jeannette, madame," said Madam Gaudet in a surprised tone.

"Thank you very much," said Sally.

CHAPTER XVII

Rue Caumartin

SALLY WENT ON DOWN the stairs into the hall. She was holding rather tightly to the handrail, but the stairs were, as Madame Gaudet had said, uneven. Charles and James Latimer, with Jeremy, were standing in the hall talking to the landlord.

"I have spoken to my wife," he was saying, "and she agrees with me that it will bring custom. It is worth it. It is not as though we believed in the nonsense."

"You are very wise," said James.

"Cash in on it," agreed Jeremy.

In the meantime, Charles had gone to the foot of the stair to meet Sally and offer his arm.

"You look a little pale this morning, ma'am," he said in a tone of concern. "Where are those lovely roses you are accustomed to wear? Did you not sleep well?"

She laid her hand upon his arm. "I slept very well, Cousin Charles, thank you." Her hand tightened. "I have just been looking at an old oil painting of a man with a black beard."

She looked straight into his eyes with a faint smile, and Charles said no word in reply. He lifted her hand and kissed it after what is still the custom on the Continent.

Jeremy came up and clapped him on the shoulder. "When you and my wife have finished spooning," he said cheerfully, "shall we get going?"

They drove away towards Paris; Sally, as usual, in the front seat next her husband and the elder Latimers behind.

"We seem to have missed some fun last night, Sally," said Jeremy. "That bunch who were also staying there are ghost-hunters."

Sally turned round eyes on him and her lips parted.

"You may well stare," said Jeremy. "It's a racket, of course. The party is run by a fellow called Popinger or some such, and I guess he's got one or two stooges in the gang. You get the room nice and dark and then throw things around and produce a few moans and wails and some mysterious blue lights. Simple. Then those mutton-headed jerks swallow it all whole and pay good money to see some more. Oh boy, what a racket!"

Sally digested this for a few moments and then turned to the occupants of the back seat.

"Did you see all this?"

"Why, yes, ma'am," said Charles. "We were much amused."

"But not very deeply impressed," said James.

"And to think we snored steadily through the whole schemozzle," said Jeremy. "I do think, Cousins, you might have come and let us in on the party."

"It was not worthy your attention," said James.

"A few simple tricks such as anyone could perform if he were a ventriloquist," said Charles.

"Imagine modern educated people being so credulous," said Jeremy. "Well, well, they say there's one born every minute."

When they stopped for lunch, Jeremy said that he and Sally were going to Luxemburg on the following day, he had to see a man there on business. Tiresome, but there it was. A man had to keep on earning his living, especially when he had a wife to keep. He smiled at Sally.

"Will you," asked James, "be passing through St. Denis-sur-Aisne?"

"Why, yes, I expect so, Cousin. It is on the direct route. We only planned to be away two or three nights and then return to Paris. St. Denis-sur-Aisne, that was where we were lucky enough to meet up with you."

"And when you come back to Paris?" asked Charles a little hoarsely. "Will you be staying in Paris for some time, if I am not intruding upon your private affairs?"

"No intrusion at all, Cousin Charles. We plan to spend two or three days in Paris and then go to England, to Sally's people, for a spell. A short spell, for I must go home. I have been over on this side, Cousin, for two years now and I anticipate with pleasure introducing my wife to my family. Dad came over for our wedding, but my mother and my sister Louella couldn't make it. It will be a great day when I take my wife home."

"I am sure," said James very kindly, "that you must be counting the days to that happy moment. I have been a widower many years now but I still recall vividly the thrill of the moment when I lifted my bride across the threshold of our home."

"Sure," said Jeremy, a little embarrassed, "sure. Well, Sally, if you're ready?"

They resumed their journey; when the car was well under way James leaned back and spoke to Charles in a low tone.

"You realize what this means, Charles. The end of the holiday."

"It has come soon," said Charles.

"This opportunity to return has been provided for us," said James. "We cannot hang about our cousins for the rest of their lives."

"No," said Charles, "no."

"Nor do we wish to drift about homeless forever, as would happen if we lost touch with them before we were safely returned home. I have been trying to devise some means of inducing them to take us back, and here it is, as I said, provided. I ought to have had more faith."

Charles, who had been leaning forward with his elbows on his knees, sat back and grinned cheerfully at James.

"You are in the right, Cousin James, as ever. We must go back. By the way, tell me, did you in fact send that money to the shopkeeper at

St. Denis-sur-Aisne? And the bank, of course?"

"Not yet," said James. "If you recall, Charles, we were only speaking of it the day before yesterday."

"Very true. It does not signify now, we can deliver the money in person." He chuckled.

"What devilment are you now contriving?" asked James with a laugh.

"No devilment at all, no, sir. Merely a little harmless amusement. I have not yet worked out the details."

"We have also to work out the details of how we are to inform our young relatives that the missing money is down the well. Your suggestion that possibly no one now knows that there ever was a well there has thoroughly alarmed me."

"There are several possible solutions to that problem, Cousin James. It will depend, in part, upon whether your priest did indeed make a note of your message. Not that it greatly signifies, we can manage quite well without it, but if there is some message still extant it would be of assistance."

"In establishing our bona-fides," nodded James.

"Precisely. We will ask Jeremy to take us with them as far as St. Denis-sur-Aisne. It is strongly advisable that they should spend the night there."

"What, exactly," said James cautiously, "had you in mind?"

"Let us go into committee upon this matter," said Charles. The cousins drew together in the back of the car and talked earnestly, in low tones, until they came into the outskirts of Paris.

Jeremy leaned back and spoke over his shoulder.

"Will you come and have dinner with us at our hotel? Sally and I would be glad if you would."

"Thank you, indeed," said James, "but Charles and I were hoping that you and Cousin Sally would honor us by having dinner with us at ours. The De Bussy is not the Ambassador by a very wide margin, but it is a decent quiet place and the cooking is good."

"Cousin James, when you talk about cooking you will find me sitting right at your feet. What about it, Sally?"

Sally smiled round at the cousins and said that she thought it was a lovely idea.

"I suppose we can park," said Jeremy, "in the Rue Caumartin?"

"People do," said Charles, "although the street is narrow. It is a—a—traffic is permitted in one direction only."

"One-way street. Which end do we go in at? Boulevard des Capucines, right? Will you pilot me, Cousin Charles?"

Charles did so, but even Jeremy was startled when they turned into the narrow twisting road which must surely be one of the oldest streets in that part of Paris.

"This is one road old Baron Haussmann didn't get down to, isn't it? I'll say it's a one-way street, it's nearly a one-car street. How far up is your hotel, for Pete's sake?"

"Only just up there," said James.

"I should stop here, if I might suggest," said Charles. "There might not be adequate space further on."

"You're telling me," said Jeremy with emphasis. He pulled in until his tires touched the pavement and they all got out.

"Now I'm blocking the sidewalk with Rollo's fenders."

"Never mind, darling," said Sally. "They all do that, look," and it was quite true.

"Pedestrians in this street," said James, "are habituated to walking sideways."

* * * *

When dinner was nearly ended James leaned across to Jeremy.

"I wonder whether we might presume so far as to ask a great favor?"

"Why, certainly," said Jeremy instantly. "Happy to do anything—what is it?"

"If you are, in fact, passing through St. Denis-sur-Aisne tomorrow, would it be imposing upon your good nature to ask you to convey us that far?"

Sally looked up sharply at Charles, who smiled back at her.

"Will you have a cigarette, Cousin Sally? Let me light it for you, ma'am."

Sally looked as though she were about to ask some question and then changed her mind.

"Thank you, Cousin Charles."

In the meantime James was explaining, a little obscurely, that they had parted with a group of friends at St. Denis on the night the Latimers had all met there, and were due to rejoin these friends very shortly. Since Jeremy was, in any case, going there tomorrow it seemed an opportunity.

"Certainly," said Jeremy in a slightly puzzled tone. "There's no doubt your friends will be there—I mean, it's rather short notice . . ." His voice trailed off.

"They will be there," said James.

"But suppose they're not, it's not much of a place to stay in," said Jeremy. "Look, why don't we stay there overnight, then if your party hasn't rolled up at least we'll have another evening together.

"A most excellent suggestion," said James approvingly, "how say you, Charles?"

"I am all in favor of it. The next day will serve equally as well to rejoin our friends."

"And Sally can get a few more hints and tips about cooking from the man who keeps the place," said Jeremy. "I'm all for my wife getting that sort of instruction. Eh, Sally? You're very quiet."

"Perhaps our fair cousin has something against the plan," said James. "Pray say, ma'am, if our coming is in any way inconvenient."

"No, no, on the contrary," said Sally quickly. "I was only sorry our party is to break up so soon. You are going away, are you?" She looked from Charles to James and back again.

"It is unfortunately unavoidable," said James. "We have—er—obligations."

"But we'll meet again one of these days," said Jeremy. "Maybe in England."

"Oh yes, we shall meet again," said Charles. "If not in England, then elsewhere, but we'll meet again."

"Sally," said Jeremy, "I do hope our cousins won't think we have no manners, but I keep sitting here wondering whether some passing truck has wiped Rollo's fenders off yet. Not the ones on the pavement, the other side."

"If you are anxious about your lovely car," said James, "it would be inhuman to detain you."

Sally got up and Charles hurried to help her into her coat.

"There's one good thing," said Jeremy, "we needn't start so early in the morning if we're only going to St. Denis. After lunch will do."

"You really do want to go to St. Denis?" said Sally over her shoulder to Charles.

"I really must, ma'am," he answered, settling the coat over her shoulders.

"Not quite the same thing," she said.

"Not quite, Cousin Sally."

"We'll walk down to the car with you," said James.

"Single file, like Indian scouts," suggested Charles.

There is, near the end of the Rue Caumartin, a small shop full of the most fascinating trifles, souvenirs of Paris of one kind and another, and Sally noticed it with delight.

"Just a minute, darling, I must look in that shop."

"Well, don't be too long, will you? Look, Sally, I'll get in the car and then if anything big comes along I'll be right on the spot."

It seemed inevitable that Charles should squire her across the road while James leaned through the car window and talked to Jeremy.

Among other things in the shop were a number of key rings such as have become popular in recent years for small gifts or as amusing souvenirs of places visited. The key ring carries a little medallion with initials upon it, or a model of the Eiffel Tower, or a St. Christopher mascot for car keys, or the symbol of a sign of the zodiac. Sally picked out one which had a reproduction of traffic lights, a small strip of brass with colored stones set in it, red, amber, and green, and also a tiny white-enamelled truncheon little more than an inch long, a miniature of the French traffic policeman's baton.

"Cousin Charles, this is a present for you, to remind you of the day you came to our rescue when we were stuck in the Boulevard des Italiens."

"Sally, my dear little cousin. You are marvelous kind to me. I shall value this and keep it always." He slipped it on one of his fingers.

"We must go," she said hastily, "or—"

She was interrupted by an outburst of hooting, for a large delivery van desired to pass the Rolls-Bentley and decided correctly that there was not enough room. Sally rushed across the road and hopped into the car, James shut the door after her, and Jeremy drove hastily away.

* * * *

They reached St. Denis-sur-Aisne the following evening and were warmly welcomed by the proprietor, who even encouraged Sally to come into his kitchen to learn how duck with oranges is prepared. André, the garage proprietor, saw the Rolls-Bentley standing outside the Hôtel du Commerce and came in to ask whether he might have the privilege and pleasure of housing the car for the night. "The garage of this hotel, monsieur, is indeed perfectly adequate. I say nothing against the garage accommodation of this hotel. It is to get into it. Let Monsieur picture to himself driving down an alley ten feet wide, turning right-handed through an archway eight feet wide, and turning again to—"

"Not too good, André, not too good," said Jeremy. "I'll be glad if you will take her and house her for the night, and look, André, we ran through rain the other side of Rheims. Would you have time—"

"To wash and polish her, monsieur; It shall be done at once, and with the utmost care. Monsieur will require her—"

"At nine tomorrow morning."

"She shall be here, monsieur."

Jeremy returned to James and Charles.

"It's a shame his garage is only fifty yards down the street. He took her at a foot pace so all his friends would see him driving her. Talking about friends, yours are not yet here?"

"Why, no," said James. "We are not, I believe, likely to see them before tomorrow morning."

Monsieur Cayeux, manager of the St. Denis-sur-Aisne branch of the Bank of France, retired to bed at his usual hour of 11 P.M., having first been all round his premises upon his usual tour to make sure that all the doors and windows were properly fastened and, as usual, they were, for he was a methodical little man. His bedroom window, like all the others in the building, had bars outside it and was closed and latched as well. Night air is dangerous in September, as everyone knows. He locked his bedroom door, got into bed, and fell asleep the moment his head was on the pillow.

Sometime very early in the small hours he dreamed a vivid dream. He was upon a small tropic island basking in the warmth. There was an incredibly blue sea, sparkling as with diamonds, spread out before him; he was sitting in the shade of palm trees-which swayed and rustled overhead. All around him was yellow sand, golden sand; he reflected that it was really the color of gold, and he could feel a pleasant grittiness as he dug his toes into it. His attention was distracted by a small dark object in the sea before him. It rose in the water and became the head of someone wading ashore; it rime ran and revealed the form of a brown-skinned girl clad only in a sarong and long masses of dark brown hair which reached her knees.

Even in sleep Cayeux was polite; he struggled to rise but found that he could not move so much as a finger. The girl came steadily on up the sand and he saw that she was holding one single, long, perfect peacock's feather.

She came right up to him, bent over him, and tickled his nose with the feather. Cayeux drew a long breath, gasped again, and sneezed so violently that he woke himself up. He was sitting upright in his own bed at home and even as he woke it seemed to him that he heard something fall off the bed with a soft thud upon the floor.

"Dear me," said Cayeux.

He looked round; the room was dimly visible by the light of a street lamp outside shining through the tin blind. It all looked exactly as usual. He sneezed again.

"I do believe," said Cayeux, "that that is the very first time I have ever dreamed in color. Technicolor," he added, logically pursuing his thought. He remembered the soft thud he had heard. "Something fell down," he said, and switched on the light. There was a white envelope upon the floor; he reached down, picked it up, and tore it open. There was money inside and a note written in an old-fashioned, pointed hand.

Borrowed, upon Sept. 4th...................................*100,375 frs:*
Interest for 2 weeks at 5 per centum per annum, approx............ <u>*250 frs:*</u>
Total....*100,625 frs:*
Monsieur, this sum was borrowed, not stolen, and is now returned with
grateful acknowledgment of the accommodation.

Cayeux clutched his hair and then counted the money. There was, indeed, one hundred thousand six hundred and twenty-five francs enclosed. He sprang out of bed and tried his bedroom door; it was still locked and the key inside. The window was still shut and latched. He clutched his hair again and returned irresolutely to bed.

"That is exactly the sum which was missing that night when the bank was broken into," he said. "It was September the fourth. I must inform my chief cashier that it has been returned. . . .

"In an envelope put on my bed in a locked room in the middle of the night. . .

"I must inform my directors.

"Peacock's feather." He rubbed his nose, for it still tingled faintly. "I *was* tickled, I can still feel it.

"I must tell my directors.

"What should I think if I were a director and one of my managers said that some missing money had unaccountably arrived on his bed in the middle of the night, together with accrued interest and a covering note?

"I know what I should think . . .

"I had much better not tell my directors, or the chief cashier either.

"I did hear noises in the strong-room before those two robbers went in with my keys. I know I did, and so did the mayor. Yet . . .

"I will not keep the money. Some charity

"I ought to tell my directors.

"I shall be a fool if I do. . . ."

CHAPTER XVIII:
Key Ring

ALPHONSE DIEUDONNÉ was a farmer like his father and grandfather before him and he farmed the same land; it was his by inheritance. It was the farm on the Sedan road out of St. Denis-sur-Aisne upon which stood the barn called the Englishmen's Barn where Jeremy Latimer's Rolls-Bentley had stopped so unaccountably that evening when he and Sally first came to St. Denis. It was, in fact, Alphonse Dieudonné who had telephoned to the St. Denis garage about the breakdown.

Upon this September night when the Latimers came to St. Denis for the second time, Dieudonné was spending the night in the barn ministering to a sick cow. Towards three o'clock in the morning the cow's misery increased so much that Dieudonné decided that he could not deal with the case himself, he must call in the veterinary surgeon, and at once. The man's charge for coming out in the middle of the night would, of course, be exorbitant, but it would be less than the value of the cow.

He came out of the barn and tramped steadily up the field towards his house. He would telephone and also make himself some coffee. Hot coffee is good at three in the morning.

He came again from his house a quarter of an hour later with some of the good coffee inside him and some more in a can which he carried. The vet would be there in half an hour to do what was necessary, the cow would then feel better, and he, Alphonse Dieudonné, could go to bed for a couple of hours.

There was no moon that night, but the skies were clear and the stars very bright; as he came near the Englishmen's Barn he saw dimly two figures standing together about ten yards from it, against the fence. They were not at all distinct and yet he saw them in the faint light; it was almost as though they had a light of their own about them. He hailed them.

"Holà! What are you doing on my land?"

The only answer was a moaning sound which, he thought, proceeded from the barn.

"Why don't you answer? Who are you?"

He had an electric torch in his pocket which he had not been using since he could see his way well enough; one does not waste batteries. He took it out and turned it upon them. They were men, tall men, and dressed in a style which even in Northern France—which is not a dressy district—looked old-fashioned. Their coats were at once too wide and too long and yet showed a great deal of waistcoat, whereas their trousers were narrow, tight, and so long that they were strapped under the boots. Dieudonné looked more closely and then noticed that the figures were semitransparent, for he could see the fence through them.

He stopped abruptly. The figures, moving exactly together, pointed down at the ground between them and slowly sank into it. When finally their heads disappeared, Dieudonné came to life. There was a clatter as

he dropped his coffee can; he ran wildly towards the gate and then only
the sound of his flying footsteps upon the road disturbed the silence of
the night. There was left only the impression, as it were, of thoughts
passing through the air.

"I thought I moaned rather well, Charles. Yet he took not the faint-
est notice."

"Alas, Cousin James, he thought it was the cow."

"What will he do now?"

"I presume he will call upon his neighbors to see this wonder. Possibly the constable."

"Indeed, I hope so, Charles. We must moan louder next time. Or
rattle chains. That is always recommended for a good effect."

There came the rattle of a loose chain from the team as the sick cow
shifted uneasily.

"Was that you, Charles?"

"No, James, no. The cow again."

"Provoking."

Some time passed, the sky began to lighten a little in the east, and
the stars turned pale. A car came along the road from Mézières and
drew up at the gate. The veterinary surgeon got out, came through the
gate, and walked along inside the fence towards the barn. When he was
about ten feet from it the two shadowy forms rose up through the ground
so close that he could have touched them if there had been anything to
touch. Once more they pointed at the ground and then sank again, but
the cow's doctor did not wait to see any more. He did not even wait to
get into his car, but ran along the road towards St. Denis until, just short
of the village, he met Dieudonné coming back accompanied by Sergeant Boulestier of the police. Dieudonné was, in fact, holding the sergeant by the arm and urging him forward.

Boulestier had almost managed to persuade himself that the sight
of the two naked men he had seen in the moonlight the night of the
bank robbery was only a dream. Nevertheless, it still remained clearly in
his mind, far too clearly. Any suggestion, therefore, that two ghosts in
manly form had been seen again was acutely distasteful to him.

"But," he said, fibbing, "if these apparitions you saw were, in fact,
supernatural, they do not come within the sphere of my authority even
though I am now a sergeant. It is not a police matter. You don't want
me, you want the priest."

"I am not," said Dieudonné, "upon such terms with the priest as to
facilitate my getting him out of bed at three in the morning to come
and look at a ghost. Even two ghosts. He would say it was a judgment on
me for not going to Mass. He would say it served me right. Whereas, if a

man in your responsible position goes to him and says there are two
ghosts by the Englishmen's Barn, he will believe you at once. Everyone
believes sergeants."

At this point, flying footsteps brought them the agitated person of
the veterinary surgeon. He seized upon the sergeant and babbled at
Dieudonné.

"There are two ghosts—"

"There," said the sergeant, halting. "There is no need for me to go
further. Here is your reliable and credible witness. Everyone believes
vets."

"Sergeant Boulestier," said Dieudonné, "permit me to tell you that
you are failing in your duty. What! A breach of the law is being commit-
ted—if ghosts aren't a breach of the law, what is—and you refuse to take
action? Do you wish to revert to the rank of constable, and you so near
your pension?"

Boulestier hesitated, heaved a sigh so deep that one would say it
began in his boots, and strode purposefully forward with Dieudonné
and the vet upon either side acting, like the Lion and the Unicorn, as
supporters. When they passed through the field gate and approached
the barn the ghosts were there waiting for them.

The ghosts were standing some six feet apart with, as it were, the
length of a grave between them. When the investigation committee arrived the ghosts paced mournfully about the grave, the taller and thinner one wringing his hands and the shorter and stouter one flinging his
arms about in gestures of despair strongly reminiscent of Irving as
Othello at Manchester in 1869. They also moaned. When, however, their
audience showed signs of immediate flight, the ghosts sank slowly and
inevitably into the ground and the first birds began to sing.

Dieudonné, emboldened by the presence of his friends, went forward and examined the spot in the growing light.

"You see?" he said. "The soil is hard and has not been disturbed, yet
they sank into it like divers. Now will you go and tell the priest, Sergeant
Boulestier? And you," to the veterinary surgeon, "to the cow!"

An hour later St. Denis-sur-Aisne was buzzing with the story and by
breakfast-time the only people in the place who had not heard it were
Sally and Jeremy Latimer.

Vigneron, the proprietor of Aristide Vigneron et Cie., departmental store, heard it from his wife, who had heard it from the postman and
the milkman. He heard it all over again, with startling embroideries,
when he opened the locked doors at the end of the arcade to admit his
shop assistants. He had to be firm, very firm indeed, before he could
induce his staff to leave off chattering and open up the shop; even then

they started again the moment his back was turned. However, since every customer who came in wanted to talk about ghosts, his staff's obsession with the subject did not really matter.

He went to his locked office and opened it; on his desk there was an envelope which had not been there the night before. It had no inscription upon it and he tore it open. It contained money, as Cayeux's envelope had done, but instead of a covering letter there were a number of small price tickets such as are attached to goods for sale. Vigneron marked his prices in plain figures, he did not use a code, but there were letters and numbers to tell him which departments were concerned. Gentlemen's outfitting, mainly, but there were a couple from the Luggage, Garden Implements, and Ironmongery and several from the Toilet Articles.

Vigneron's mind went back to two suits, hats, suitcases, and other items missing a fortnight earlier. He looked wildly round him.

"But the place was all locked up," he said, and thought for a moment.

"But I have been repaid," he added, and checked the money against the tickets. It was correct.

"All the same," he said firmly, "these locks shall be changed. All of them. Today."

* * * *

"Our cousins," said Jeremy, "have overslept." He looked at his watch. "It's ten minutes to nine and I'd like to get away before long. I wonder whether they asked to be called at any particular hour."

"Ask the landlord," suggested Sally, pouring the last of the coffee into Jeremy's cup. "I'd like another roll if there's time, and isn't this lovely butter?"

"Don't rush it, honey, there's always time to do what you want." Jeremy got up from the breakfast table, put his head through the service door, had a few words with the landlord, and came back.

"He says no, but he'll go up and see if they are about."

The landlord came to the dining-room door a few minutes later and said: "Excuse me, monsieur—"

Jeremy went out with him into the hall and said, "What is it?"

"Not to alarm Madame, but they are not there, monsieur."

"Not there? I suppose they have gone for a walk."

"Not unless they have gone out with no clothes on, monsieur."

"Oh, don't be absurd," said Jeremy, and Sally came to the door to say, "What is it?"

"Our cousins have gone out early," said Jeremy. "I guess they'll be right back."

"Monsieur—madame—their beds have not been slept in, their suit-cases have not been unfastened, and their clothes are all there neatly folded upon chairs and the shoes standing under the chairs. Even their hats are there."

"They never went a yard outside without their hats," said Jeremy. "Did they, Sally?"

"No," agreed Sally in a small voice, and Jeremy put his arm round her.

"Now don't get all het up, honey, there's some simple explanation. Maybe they went out to buy some new hats and they'll come walking in with them."

"But their clothes," said the landlord.

"You're mistaken, that's all. What about their bedroom key?"

"It was not in the lock and the door was not fastened," said the landlord. He turned towards his little office, a small compartment in the hall with glass panels in its door.

"There you are," said Jeremy, "they have gone out and taken it with them," but the landlord was peering through the glass panels of the door at the numbered keyboard on the wall. He took a bunch of keys from his pocket, unlocked the office door, and went in.

He came out again with the; key in one hand and some notes in the other.

"This is the key of their room, number five. There were also these two thousand-franc notes folded up and thrust through the bow of the key, to pay their bills, no doubt."

"Well, now you're all right, aren't you?" said Jeremy. "What are you looking so bothered about?"

"How did they get into my office, monsieur? The door was locked last night and I have only opened it this moment. It is a good lock, extra-good, and I have the only key."

"You forgot to lock it," said Jeremy stoutly.

"Then how came it to be locked just now, monsieur?"

"How soon was this hotel opened up this morning?" asked Jeremy, abandoning the lock argument as unprofitable. "Maybe somebody saw them go."

"I will enquire," said the landlord, and went into the kitchen quarters.

"Don't look so white, sweetie," said Jeremy. "I guess their friends called in early and took them out someplace. They'll be along any moment now to tell us good-bye and pick up their bags. Come and have some more coffee."

"There isn't any more," said Sally.

"Then they can bring some," said Jeremy. "Come and sit down. Oh, here's André with Rollo."

André ame in and wished them good morning. "The car is all ready, if Monsieur is satisfied with her appearance."

Jeremy began to say that no doubt she was perfectly all right, but Sally interrupted him.

"André. Did the car start easily this morning?"

André stared. "But perfectly, madame. Ah, I have it, you are remembering the time she stopped by the Englishmen's Barn, but that was only the batt—"

"The what did you say?" asked Sally breathlessly.

"The battery terminals, madame."

"No, no. You mentioned some barn."

"The Englishmen's Barn, madame. That tumble-down building where your car stopped before. That is its name."

"Why is it called that?"

"I could not say, madame." André broke into a laugh. "There were some fine doings by the Englishmen's Barn this morning, by all accounts."

"What happened?" asked Jeremy.

"Monsieur Alphonse Dieudonné, he lives at the farmhouse there and farms that land—"

"I guess we met him," said Jeremy. "Wasn't it he who rang through for you to come and get us?"

"That is right, monsieur. It seems he was at the barn all night with a sick cow and there were two ghosts there."

There was a wooden settle in the hall. Sally sat down upon it with an almost audible bump and Jeremy said: "Well, if that doesn't beat the band. A farmer seeing ghosts. Was he celebrating last night? Had a birthday, or something?"

"I could not say, monsieur. He is in the town telling everybody about it and saying something ought to be done."

"Well, what would you do about ghosts? Get the priest to talk to them, or what?"

"He says they said they were buried there and they want to be dug up and buried in consecrated ground."

"So they talked to him, did they?" asked Jeremy.

"Not in words, it seems, monsieur. He says he knew what they were thinking."

"He's a thought-reader, huh?"

"André," said Sally, "these ghosts, what did they look like, do you know?"

"No, madame, I did not ask him."

Jeremy lost interest.

"I suppose this is all most interesting to the local inhabitants," he said, "but what I want is to say good-bye to our cousins and get on. Guess I'll go out in the street, maybe I'll see them coming."

André went outside to look up and down the street.

"I don't think you will," said Sally.

"Don't think I will? For Pete's sake, why not?"

The landlord came back and said that it was manifestly impossible for the Messieurs Latimer to have left the hotel unseen after the doors were unlocked in the morning. The cleaning women had been here, his wife there, and he himself somewhere else all the time. The fact is that small French provincial hotels are mistrustful places; guests who show signs of slipping away early would certainly be seen.

"Well, they've gone, haven't they?" said Jeremy impatiently. "You don't suggest that they are hiding under the beds, do you?"

"I have looked," said the landlord simply.

"Well, there you are. Look, honey, I can't hang about. I'll write a little note to our cousins and they can have it when they come back—"

"Certainly, monsieur," said the landlord. "There is writing paper in my office, I will bring—"

"Let me write in there," said Jeremy. "It's only to scribble a line."

The landlord settled him in and returned to Sally.

"Tell me," she said, "this Englishmen's Barn, do you know why it is called that?"

"There has always been a story in the village, madame, that when the Germans came through here, after Sedan, on their way to Paris, that was in 1870, madame—"

"Yes, yes—"

"That they shot two Englishmen and a monkey—"

Sally's hands flew up to her mouth.

"That is the story, madame, and that they were all buried by that barn. Now Dieudonné and others have seen them and told the curé and the curé says that he has some old writing in a book about them, written by the curé who was here at that time. That is, in 1870, madame. So it seems that the story must be true, at least about the men; as for the monkey, I cannot say."

Jeremy returned, sticking down the flap of the envelope addressed to Messieurs James and Charles Latimer.

"What's all this about monkeys?"

"Tell my husband," said Sally to the landlord, "what you have just told me."

The landlord repeated his story word for word.

"Were you thinking, honey, that these might be our missing ancestors?"

Sally nodded.

Jeremy considered this.

"What are they doing about all this?" he asked.

"Digging, monsieur. The curé says that if human remains are found he will give them Christian burial. It is not right, he says, that Christian men should lie buried in the edge of a field like a dead dog."

"No," said Jeremy thoughtfully, "no. And he has some writing about it, you say? Honey, I think I'd best wire to Luxemburg and say I'll be delayed. We should go see this curé; the writing might say who they were. If they were our ancestors, we can't have them buried by the parish."

"There's the monkey, too," said Sally. "Charles Latimer's monkey. There couldn't be two sets of two-Englishmen-and-a-monkey getting lost in 1870."

"I remember," said Jeremy, "you told me about the monkey. One of them was Charles, was he? What was the other one's name, do you know?"

"James."

"Oh, was it? Are you sure? What an odd coincidence."

Sally looked at him, opened her mouth to speak, and shut it again.

"Well," said Jeremy, "shall we go see this curé? Maybe he'll know the Englishmen's names were Smith, or some such, and then we can push off to Luxemburg after all."

The curé was a stout elderly man with a round cheerful face and the Latimers took to him on sight. Jeremy explained why they were taking an interest in this affair, "though all this ghost business is a bit beyond me. Father, what do you reckon Dieudonné and the others saw?"

"Ghosts, my son, ghosts. It is not an unheard of thing for aggrieved spirits to appear and demand their rights. These men were, it seems, denied Christian burial and they are right to demand it. It is a common motive for the appearance of ghosts. There is only one thing that puzzles me—"

"What is that?" asked Sally.

"Why wait till now? They have lain quietly enough, it seems, for over eighty years. But who are we to question?"

"This writing," said Jeremy.

"Certainly." The priest went to an oak chest in a corner of the room and unlocked it. "I read it many years ago, when I first came here; I was about to get it out again when you came." He lifted out musty old volumes of birth, marriage, and death registers and records of church accounts. "It is in the burials register for that time. This is it."

He laid the book upon the table and opened it. "1865. Too early. 1868. Further on still. 1869. 1870, ah. But what—"

As he turned the page an envelope slipped out, a new, clean envelope with a name and address written upon it. "Mrs. Sally Latimer, Oakwood Hall, Didsbury, England," in a slanting, pointed hand. The curé read it aloud.

"That—that's my wife," gasped Jeremy.

"The letter is for me," said Sally steadily, and held out her hand, but the curé retained the letter.

"I beg a thousand pardons, madame, but this is a very curious affair. You have, no doubt, some proof of your identity?"

"Show him our passport, darling."

Jeremy obeyed.

"Thank you, madame. Here is your letter."

Sally opened it and read it.

St. Denis-sur-Aisne
18th September 1953

My dear Sally,

If you dig in the north corner of the stable-yard at Oakwood Hall you will find the well referred to in my original message. I presume the money is still there.

That you may be always prosperous, happy, and, above all, kind and good, is the profound hope of

Your affectionate Gt-Grandfather
James Latimer

She passed it to Jeremy and the curé, who read it together, and the curé bent his head and crossed himself reverently.

"Now the original message," said Jeremy in stunned voice, and the curé read it out.

"2nd September 1870

"This day the Prussians came. They shot, by Dieudonnés' farm, Gustav Meunnier, waiter, of this parish, two Englishmen, names unknown, and their monkey, a pet. Gustav Meunier we were permitted to bury in our churchyard, but the Englishmen were buried where they fell and the body of the animal thrown also into the pit.

"One Englishman and Meunier were already dead when I reached the spot but I was permitted to speak to the other. He left this message: If

any should come to enquire for us, bid them look where Truth is said to dwell. *I asked his name but he had no time to answer.*

"*Signed, Camille Tallin, Curé*"

There was dead silence for some moments.

"Madame," said the curé suddenly, "a glass of wine, you are white and shaken. I beg of you to calm yourself." He bustled to a cupboard and brought out thick plain glasses and a bottle of the local white wine. "Pray, madame, drink this. Monsieur also?"

"Yes, please," said Jeremy, who appeared to be entangled in confused thoughts. He swallowed the contents of the glass and absent-mindedly held it out to be refilled. The curé did so.

"I do not understand," began Jeremy in French, and then abandoned that hampering language for his native tongue. "I don't get it; Sally, what is all this? Is this someone playing a joke on us?"

"No," said Sally. "Oh, darling, can't you see?"

"No, I don't. Who wrote that note?"

"Cousin James Latimer."

"What, the one that's been touring around with us? Why, I always said they were a pair of jokers. They're no slouches at opening locks either, are they?"

"Jeremy. Do you remember the bartender at the Ambassador telling us he'd seen a vanishing monkey? That's when I began to see what they were. I was scared, but Cousin Charles was so sweet, he came and told me not to be frightened, and I never was after that."

"Are you trying to tell me that we've been cavorting about France with a brace of ghosts?"

Sally nodded and her eyes slowly filled with tears.

"I don't believe it," said Jeremy obstinately. "Why, they were as solid as you and I."

"There's only one thing," said Sally. "Here's a message from Great-grandfather James, but not a word from Cousin Charles. I thought Cousin Charles—"

She was interrupted by a thundering knock on the priest's front door; with a murmured excuse he went to answer it, leaving the door of the sitting-room open. It was impossible to avoid overhearing the loud country voice outside.

"Monsieur le Curé, they was there all right. We dug down careful and there they was. Only bones, you understand, but doctor says as they was two piggish men. There was some small bones, too, looked like a child's, but doctor, he examines 'em and says no, it's a monkey."

"Inform the undertaker," said the curé's calm voice, "let them be reverently coffined. I will myself come and see that it is properly done, decently and in order."

"And the monkey? You won't put monkey in consecrate ground, surely?"

"Certainly not, but the animal shall be buried just outside the cemetery wall."

"Also, monsieur, we found this among the bones. The taller one had had a finger through it, I took it off myself. Don't seem to belong, do it?"

"Give it to me," said the curé, "I will take charge of it. Go now and order two coffins."

The door shut and the priest returned to Sally and Jeremy; he had some small object in a clasped hand.

"We couldn't help overhearing," said Sally apologetically.

"My good Dompierre has a deaf wife," said the priest, "so he bellows at everyone." He looked at his closed hand.

"What did they find?" asked Jeremy. "A signet ring, perhaps? That might prove—"

"Not a signet ring," said the curé and laid a key ring upon the table, a bright new key ring bearing emblems of Paris traffic; stop-and-go lights and a policeman's white truncheon.

THE END

Rue Morgue Press titles as of March 2000

The Black-Heade Pins by Constance & Gwenyth Little. "...a zany, fun-loving puzzler spun by the sisters Little—it's celluloid screwball comedy printed on paper. The charm of this book lies in the lively banter between characters and the breakneck pace of the story. You hardly grasp how the first victim was done in when you have to grapple with outlandish clues like two black-headed pins."—Diane Plumley, *Dastardly Deeds*.With her bank account down to empty, orphaned Leigh Smith has no choice but to take a job as a paid companion and housekeeper to the miserly Mrs. Ballister. However, once she moves into the drafty, creaking old Ballister mansion in the wilds of New Jersey, Smithy has reason to regret her decision. But when Mrs. Ballister decides to invite her nieces and nephews for Christmas, Smithy sees the possibility for some fun. What she doesn't expect is to encounter the Ballister family curse. It seems that when a dragging noise is heard in the attic it foretells the death of a Ballister. And once a Ballister dies, if you don't watch the body until it's buried, it's likely to walk. The stockings are barely hung from the mantle when those dreaded sounds are heard in the attic, and before long, corpses are going for regular midnight strolls. Smithy and a pair of potential beaux turn detective and try to figure out why the murderer leaves black-headed pins at the scene of every crime. Filled with the eccentric characters and odd plot twists typical of a Little mystery, *The Black-Headed Pins* first appeared in 1938 and was the second book by the two queens of the wacky cozy. **0-915230-25-9** **$14.00**

The Black Gloves by Constance & Gwenyth Little. "I'm relishing every madcap moment."—*Murder Most Cozy*. Welcome to the Vickers estate near East Orange, New Jersey, where the middle class is destroying the neighborhood, erecting their horrid little cottages, playing on the Vickers tennis court, and generally disrupting the comfortable life of Hammond Vickers no end. It's bad enough that he had to shell out good money to his daughter Lissa a Reno divorce only to have her brute of an ex-husband show up on his doorstep. But why does there also have to be a corpse in the cellar? And lights going on and off in the attic? First published in 1939. **0-915230-20-8** **$14.00**

The Black Honeymoon by Constance & Gwenyth Little. Can you murder someone with feathers? If you don't believe feathers are lethal, then you probably haven't read a Little mystery. No, Uncle Richard wasn't tickled to death—though we can't make the same guarantee for readers—but the hyper-allergic rich man did manage to sneeze himself into the hereafter in his hospital room. Suspicion falls on his nurse, young Miriel Mason, who recently married the dead man's nephew, an army officer on furlough. To clear herself of murder as well as charges of being a gold-digger, Miriel summons private detective Kelly, an old crony of her father's, who gets himself hired as a servant even though he can't cook, clean or serve. First published in 1944. **0-915230-21-6** **$14.00**

Great Black Kanba by Constance & Gwenyth Little. "If you love train mysteries as much as I do, hop on the Trans-Australia Railway in *Great Black Kanba*, a fast and funny 1944 novel by the talented (Littles)."—Jon L. Breen, *Ellery Queen's Mystery Magazine*. "I have decided to add *Kanba* to my favorite mysteries of all time list!...a zany ride I'll definitely take again and again."—Diane Plumley in the Murder Ink newsletter. When a young American woman wakes up on an Australia train with a bump on her head and no memory, she suddenly finds out that she's engaged to two different men and the chief suspect in a murder case. But she's almost more upset to discover that she appears to have absolutely dreadful taste in clothing. It all adds up to some delightful mischief—call it Cornell Woolrich on laughing gas. **0-915230-22-4** **$14.00**

The Grey Mist Murders by Constance & Gwenyth Little. Who—or what—is the mysterious figure that emerges from the grey mist to strike down several passengers on the final leg of a round-the-world sea voyage? Is it the same shadowy entity that persists in leaving three matches outside Lady Marsh's cabin every morning? And why does one flimsy negligee seem to pop up at every turn? When Carla Bray first heard things go bump in the night, she hardly expected to find a corpse in the adjoining cabin. Nor did she expect to find herself the chief suspect in the murders. Robert Arnold, a sardonic young man who joined the ship in Tahiti, makes a play for Carla but if he's really interested in helping to clear her of murder, why does he spend so much time courting other women on board? This 1938 effort was the Littles' first book. **0-915230-26-7** **$14.00**

Murder is a Collector's Item by Elizabeth Dean. "(It) froths over with the same effervescent humor as the best Hepburn-Grant films."—Sujata Massey. "Completely enjoyable."—*New York Times.* "Fast and funny."—*The New Yorker.* Twenty-six-year-old Emma Marsh isn't much at spelling or geography and perhaps she butchers the odd literary quotation or two, but she's a keen judge of character and more than able to hold her own when it comes to selling antiques or solving murders. When she stumbles upon the body of a rich collector on the floor of the Boston antiques shop where she works, suspicion quickly falls upon her missing boss. Emma knows Jeff Graham is no murderer, but veteran homicide copy Jerry Donovan doesn't share her convictions, and Emma enlists the aid of Hank Fairbanks, her wealthy boyfriend and would-be criminologist, to nab the real killer. Originally published in 1939, *Murder is a Collector's Item* was the first of three books featuring Emma. Smoothly written and sparkling with dry, sophisticated humor, this nearly forgotten milestone combines an intriguing puzzle with an entertaining portrait of a self-possessed young woman on her own in Boston toward the end of the Great Depression. **0-915230-19-4** **$14.00**

Murder is a Serious Business by Elizabeth Dean. It's 1940 and the Thirsty Thirties are over but you couldn't tell it by the gang at J. Graham Antiques where clerk Emma Marsh, her would-be criminologist boyfriend Hank, and boss Jeff Graham trade barbs in between shots of scotch when they aren't bothered by the rare customer. Trouble starts when Emma and crew head for a weekend at Amos Currier's country estate to inventory the man's antiques collection. It isn't long before the bodies start falling and once again Emma is forced to turn sleuth in order to prove that her boss isn't a killer. Emma is sure there's a good reason why Jeff didn't mention that he had Amos' 18th century silver muffineer hidden in his desk drawer back at the shop. Filled with the same clever dialog and eccentric characters that made *Murder is a Collector's Item* an absolute delight, this second case offers up an unusual approach to crime solving as well as a sidesplitting look at the peculiar world of antiques. **0-915230-28-3** **$14.95**

Murder, Chop Chop by James Norman. "The book has the butter-wouldn't-melt-in-his-mouth cool of Rick in *Casablanca.*"—*The Rocky Mountain News.* "Amuses the reader no end."—*Mystery News.* "This mystery-thriller combo has a distinctive period flavor without a dated feel."—Nina King, *Washington Post* Book Review editor in *Crimes of the Scene.* "This long out-of-print masterpiece is intricately plotted, full of eccentric characters and very humorous indeed. Highly recommended."—*Mysteries by Mail.* Meet Gimiendo Hernandez Quinto, a gigantic Mexican who once rode with Pancho Villa and who now trains *guerrilleros* for the Nationalist Chinese government when he isn't solving murders. At his side is a beautiful Eurasian known as Mountain of Virtue, a woman as dangerous to men as she is irresistible. Then there's Mildred Woodford, a hard-drinking British journalist; John Tate, a portly American calligrapher who wasn't made for adventure; Lieutenant Chi, a young Hunanese patriot weighted down with the cares of China and the Brooklyn Dodgers; and a host of others, anyone of whom may have killed Abe Harrow, an ambulance driver who appears to have died at three different times. There's also a cipher or two to crack, a train with a mind of its own, and Chiang Kai-shek's false teeth, which have gone mysteriously missing. First published in 1942.   **0-915230-16-X $13.00**

Death at The Dog by Joanna Cannan. "Worthy of being discussed in the same breath with an Agatha Christie or Josephine Tey...anyone who enjoys Golden Age mysteries will surely enjoy this one."—Sally Fellows, *Mystery News*. "Skilled writing and brilliant characterization."—*Times of London*. "An excellent English rural tale."—Jacques Barzun & Wendell Hertig Taylor in *A Catalogue of Crime*. Set in late 1939 during the first anxious months of World War II, *Death at The Dog*, which was first published in 1941, is a wonderful example of the classic English detective novel that first flourished between the two World Wars. Set in a picturesque village filled with thatched-roof-cottages, eccentric villagers and genial pubs, it's as well-plotted as a Christie, with clues abundantly and fairly planted, and as deftly written as the best of the books by either Sayers or Marsh, filled with quotable lines and perceptive observations on the human condition. Cannan had a gift for characterization that's second to none in Golden Age detective fiction, and she created two memorable lead characters. One of them is Inspector Guy Northeast, a lonely young Scotland Yard inspector who makes his second and final appearance here and finds himself hopelessly smitten with the chief suspect in the murder of a village tyrant. The other is the "lady novelist" Cressy Hardwick, an unconventional and ultimately unobtainable woman a number of years guy's senior, who is able to pierce his armor and see the unhappiness that haunts the detective's private moments. Well aware that all the evidence seems to point to her, she is also able—unlike her less imaginative fellow villagers—to see how very good Northeast is at his job.   **0-915230-23-2 $14.00**

They Rang Up the Police by Joanna Cannan. "Just Delightful."—*Sleuth of Baker Street* Pick-of-the-Month. "A brilliantly plotted mystery...splendid character study...don't miss this one, folks. It's a keeper."—Sally Fellows, *Mystery News*. When Delia Cathcart and Major Willoughby disappear from their quiet English village one Saturday morning in July 1937, it looks like a simple case of a frustrated spinster running off for a bit of fun with a straying husband. But as the hours turn into days, Inspector Guy Northeast begins to suspect that she may have been the victim of foul play. On the surface, Delia appeared to be a quite ordinary middle-aged Englishwoman content to spend her evenings with her sisters and her days with her beloved horses. But Delia led a secret life—and Guy turns up more than one person who would like to see Delia dead. Except Delia wasn't the only person with a secret...Never published in the United States, *They Rang Up the Police* appeared in England in 1939.   **0-915230-27-5 $14.00**

Cook Up a Crime by Charlotte Murray Russell. "Perhaps the mother of today's "cozy" mystery...amateur sleuth Jane has a personality guaranteed to entertain the most demanding reader."—Andy Plonka, *The Mystery Reader*. "Some wonderful old time recipes...highly recommended."—*Mysteries by Mail*. Meet Jane Amanda Edwards, a self-styled "full-fashioned" spinster who complains she hasn't looked at herself in a full-length mirror since Helen Hokinson started drawing for *The New Yorker*. But you can always count on Jane to look into other people's affairs, especially when there's a juicy murder case to investigate. In this 1951 title Jane goes searching for recipes (included between chapters) for a cookbook project and finds a body instead. And once again her lily-of-the-field brother Arthur goes looking for love, finds strong drink, and is eventually discovered clutching the murder weapon.   **0-915230-18-6 $13.00**

The Man from Tibet by Clyde B. Clason. Locked inside the Tibetan Room of his Chicago luxury apartment, the rich antiquarian was overheard repeating a forbidden occult chant under the watchful eyes of Buddhist gods. When the doors were opened it appeared that he had succumbed to a heart attack. But the elderly Roman historian and sometime amateur sleuth Theocritus Lucius Westborough is convinced that Adam Merriweather's death was anything but natural and that the weapon was an eighth century Tibetan manuscript. It it's murder, who could have done it, and how? Suspects abound. There's's Tsongpun Bonbo, the gentle Tibetan lama from whom the manuscript was originally stolen; Chang, Merriweather's scholarly Tibetan secretary who had fled a Himalayan monastery; Merriweather's son Vincent, who disliked his father and stood to inherit a fortune; Dr. Jed Merriweather, the dead man's brother, who came to Chicago to beg for funds to continue his archaeological digs in Asia; Dr. Walters, the dead man's physician, who guarded a secret; and Janice Shelton, his young ward, who found herself being pushed by Merriweather into marrying his son. How the murder was accomplished has earned praise from such impossible crime connoisseurs as Robert C.S. Adey, who cited Clason's "highly original and practical locked-room murder method."   **0-915230-17-8** **$14.00**

The Mirror by Marlys Millhiser. "Completely enjoyable."—*Library Journal* . "A great deal of fun."—*Publishers Weekly.* How could you not be intrigued, as one reviewer pointed out, by a novel in which "you find the main character marrying her own grandfather and giving birth to her own mother?" Such is the situation in Marlys Millhiser's classic novel (a Mystery Guild selection originally published by Putnam in 1978) of two women who end up living each other's lives after they look into an antique Chinese mirror. Twenty-year-old Shay Garrett is not aware that she's pregnant and is having second thoughts about marrying Marek Weir when she's suddenly transported back 78 years in time into the body of Brandy McCabe, her own grandmother, who is unwillingly about to be married off to miner Corbin Strock. Shay's in shock but she still recognizes that the picture of her grandfather that hangs in the family home doesn't resemble her husband-to-be. But marry Corbin she does and off she goes to the high mining town of Nederland, where this thoroughly modern young woman has to learn to cope with such things as wood cooking stoves and—to her—old-fashioned attitudes about sex. In the meantime, Brandy McCabe is finding it even harder to cope with life in the Boulder, Co., of 1978.   **0-915230-15-1**   **$14.95**

Death on Milestone Buttress by Glyn Carr. When Shakespearean actor/manager Abercrombie Lewker heads for Wales for a bit of scrambling on Tryfan mountain, he hardly expects that he'll have to turn detective and figure out who killed a very disagreeable young man while he was still roped to his climbing companion on one of Tryfan's easier routes, the Milestone Buttress. Carr lovingly recreates the Welsh countryside and works climbing lore into this cunningly crafted representative of the impossible crime school of detective fiction. Set in 1947 and first published in 1951, *Death on Milestone Buttress* was the first of 15 climbing mysteries written by Carr. Available March 2000.   **0-915230-29-1**   **$14.00**

About The Rue Morgue Press

The Rue Morgue Press vintage mystery line is designed to bring back into print those books that were favorites of readers between the turn of the century and the 1960s. The editors welcome suggestions for reprints. To receive our catalog or make suggestions, write The Rue Morgue Press, P.O. Box 4119, Boulder, Colorado 80306.